Badge, Bond & Blood

A Sara O'Shea Mystery

by

Dee Wooldridge

Dedication

I dedicate this novel to my wife and family for their continuing support of my dreams. This book is especially for my granddaughters. As they venture through their lives, may they each be brave, tenacious and strong and follow their dreams. May they become a reflection of the traits of Sara O'Shea and of Becca.

Search for what is good and strong and beautiful in your society and elaborate from there. Push outward. Always create from what you already have. Then you will know what to do.

Michel Foucault

Contents

Chapter One

Lakeland, Florida

Sara O'Shea thought, "Florida isn't Missouri." Temperatures and the thermometer's mercury rose even faster than the sun above the horizon. To Sara, it felt as if they were mere inches from the fiery orb. The Floridian humidity seemed to create a hydroponic disaster under her arms and in any other place it could, every time she stepped into the sun. How could it be this hot in February? They weren't in Kansas City anymore; it wasn't home.

The spectators in the bleachers buzzed and shouted. The noise from the Lakeland neighborhoods and the incessant traffic on Interstate 4 created a near-spectral rumble beyond the event field. With the multitude of dogs barking, Police Sergeant O'Shea revisited her discomfort and her desire simply to get back on regular duty with her partner in the vastly cooler environment of KC.

Sara sat comparatively comfortably in the event tent's shade; the tent supplied by the Lakeland Police Department. She sipped bottled water and watched the competition and the rest of the city through the smoky lenses of the lo-drag ballistic sunglasses. Her partner lay beside her in the grass under the tent, her back pressed against the aluminum of the folding chair. She occasionally lapped water from the cooling bowl. Sara draped her hand over the armrest, and her partner touched her fingertips with a wet nose.

"Yeah, I know," Sara whispered.

Other law enforcement officers around her tended to mingle, sometimes trying to get too close. They considered the event week a vacation. Sara only wanted to get home, even if she'd need to trade her tactical shorts for thermal underwear. She wore a polo shirt with the KCMPD embroidered badge with her sergeant markings. Sara wore a duty belt with the Sig Sauer 9mm P226 holstered. The ball cap snug over her sunglasses hid her features, while her braided hair poked through the back of the cap. She wasn't interested in getting to know the competition.

Her partner stirred, and her tail thudded against the lawn chair's leg once, alerting Sara to someone's approach.

"Sergeant O'Shea, you and Becca are up for the next event," the young man said. He waited, expecting Sara to respond. When it didn't happen, he slipped away. Becca's tail thumped once.

Sara tightened the bottle cap and stood. Becca was up, pressing her shoulder against Sara's knee. She looked down while Becca looked up at her, panting.

"Are you ready to kick their asses?" she asked.

Becca chuffed, as if answering the question in the affirmative.

The last event after three days was the one that mattered. The two days leading up to the final round pitted Becca against top law enforcement K9 officers nationwide. Becca was the only female officer in the national competition.

Spectators, mainly composed of law enforcement families and police wannabes, sat in the bleachers under a metal awning. The other handlers and judges sat in a variety of chairs or stood pacing in the heat, lining the side of the field. The public almost never attended the event, which was fine. Why give away all the K9-handling secrets to potential criminal elements?

The USPCA Region One competition happens annually in Lakeland. It was Becca's first time, and Sara did not consider it significant. Still, Lieutenant Charlie Bertrand, her superior officer, and the Kansas City Police Chief decided it was good PR for the department and all six patrol divisions.

"Are you ready, Sergeant O'Shea?" the coordinator asked.

"Yes, sir," she said before asking, "Did the Chips K9 ever come back?"

The coordinator chuckled and nodded. "Yes, ma'am, they caught the 'perp' over by the municipal park. We think it was an inside job by the Lakeland boys."

On day one, during the obedience course, the California Highway Patrol's K9 bolted when an errant pigeon landed on one of the orange cones and chased it out of the area.

The obedience course comprised three exercises: controlling attitudes between handler and K9, heeling controls, walking controls, and distance control through various hand signals and commands. These show the judges how well dogs understand their surroundings and how well their handlers deal with gestures and communication.

For Becca, it was nothing more than the same motions she made with Sara almost every week. From a spectator's vantage point, it might have looked like Becca was more of a robot dog, pre-pro-grammed or bored going through the routines.

In the last portion of the obedience exercise, the K9s responded to hand signals and to voice commands from a minimum of 50 feet and was where nearly all dogs lost most of the competition points. Becca's favorite part is when the K9 must stop halfway, sit or lie down, and then attack.

The team needed to score at least 70% of 120 points to continue. Becca received full marks, while the ChiP's dog ran after the terrorist pigeon.

"You can begin," the coordinator said.

Sara nodded once and stepped over the line for the last event. Becca kept pace, right at Sara's side. Becca watched the surroundings, watched Sara, and mostly wanted to have fun.

Day two of the competition already knocked out five more teams from the finals. Suspect Search consisted of searching six containers large enough to fit a human. Six containers randomly scattered across the field contained contaminants from human scent prior to searches. The idea was to fool the dog into thinking they got the correct box when it was only a warm box from lingering odors.

The K9 has four minutes to search the six boxes and indicate which still has a person and not dirty underwear or lingering fart odors. Competition is fierce. With the secret handshake or prior membership to the good 'ol boys' club, someone might advance to article searches in under a few minutes. Sometimes, men hiding in boxes carried dog treats and left them behind. Becca completed the container search in record time, sprinting to each box and returning to the one containing the person in the box.

Unlike other K9 teams, Becca exhibited an acute sense of her sur-roundings during the Article Search. The competition allowed K9s three minutes to search a thirty-by-thirty-foot area of high grass. Dogs were required to retrieve either a key on a single ring or a rubber handgun.

Before Becca's turn, Sara crouched beside her and whispered, "It's hot out here. If you get this done quickly, I'll buy you an ice cream."

Becca found the gun first *and* returned to get the key in just shy of two minutes. The judges discussed Sara's tactics, questioning why she hadn't accompanied her K9 on the field. Typically, handlers were out there with the dog but only gave commands.

Sara only shrugged and said, "I would have only gotten in her way."

They approached the lines and cones designated for the final round of the K9 competition. Becca pressed her shoulder against Sara's leg as she walked. When she stopped, Becca sat. Sara glanced around the open area. Becca only watched Sara, oblivious to the surroundings or uninterested, until Sara told Becca to notice something.

The coordinator signaled to Sara to begin. Sara glanced down, smiling at Becca.

"Alright, let's show them," Sara said.

At three years old, Becca was a purebred Belgian Malinois. Standing twenty-four inches high, she weighed 54 lbs. during the competition. Her hair coat was short, straight, and weather-resistant, with a dense undercoat. The overlay was fawn in contrast to her muzzle. Her deep brown eyes complemented her black muzzle. Becca was robust, quick, and, once in motion, stayed that way. She was swift in assessing situations to protect Sara.

Becca completed more obligatory academy training than Sara when she joined the KCMPD. Firearm training, tactical responses, bomb and drug classes, and as much field gear as Sara wore when she went on patrol. Sometimes, Becca wore special UV sunglasses with ear protection when Sara brought her to the firing range, so Becca got used to the tense atmosphere.

Her ancestors were one of four varieties of Belgian herding dogs before becoming an official breed in the United States in 1959. Becca was brilliant and observant. She could chase down a fleeing suspect or herd a gaggle of geese with the same enthusiasm. Becca was sleek instead of bulky. She wasn't looking for attention; she only wanted to keep moving.

Some of Becca's cousins did tandem parachuting on military missions, including the Seal Team Six mission that ended Osama bin Laden's life.

Becca could scale a ten-foot fence with no effort. She'd tracked a suspect up a fire escape and rooftop once and managed to climb the ladder, scale the retaining wall, and catch the guy before he could grab a brick to bash her head.

Under the Florida sun, Sara gave Becca her first command gesture on the field for the criminal apprehension event. The last portion consisted of five events. In the False Start event, Sara and Becca remained immobile while a contact suspect jolted away. Becca watched Sara, waiting for the command. But since Sara didn't pursue the suspect, neither did Becca.

In the Recall event, Becca bolted after the fleeing suspect, but Sara called her back after Becca ran 20 yards. Since Becca ran at nearly 35 mph, as she got further away from Sara, the sound intensity decreased, potentially below the dog's hearing threshold. Sara'd practiced the event several times leading up to the competition and knew she would need to give the "STOP" command earlier than the 20-yard threshold. Becca always went too fast from the go command to the stop command. She ran over 5 yards beyond the stop line before trotting back to Sara's side.

The Straight Apprehension allowed Becca to get her teeth into a suspect. Becca's reflexes were lightning-fast. She was quick to bite and enjoyed it. With a bite force of 195 PSI, when Becca bit someone, they immediately noticed.

During a routine traffic stop last summer, Sara watched a suspect performing a field sobriety test in front of his car. Becca waited patiently inside the patrol SUV. While Sara focused on the sobriety test, a tall, red-haired man approached from the rear passenger side of the vehicle. He held a knife and meant to attack Sara from behind as the DUI suspect failed his test.

Becca leaped out the open window and snatched the man's arm, cracking bone and garnishing the would-be cop killer with seventeen stitches. Becca got a commendation, and the DUI suspect and his accomplice went to prison. The computers flagged both men with outstanding warrants from other states.

Sara signaled Becca to attack the suspect during the Straight Apprehension. Becca bolted and leaped, surprising the poor volunteer police officer. He expected a ground assault. He got a cruise missile. As he raised the padded sleeve to protect his face and neck, Becca anticipated the arm; her jaws gaped and snapped shut as soon as he presented it. He was off-balance, falling when Sara commanded Becca to release. The officer landed on his back; Becca let go of his arm as soon as she landed all four paws on top of him and trotted happily back to Sara's side.

The judges conferred for some time after the demonstration because Becca performed her duty, releasing the suspect on command, but when she sauntered back to Sara's side, it was glib instead of protection mode. Sara contained her smile quickly, hiding it under the cap.

"Show off," she whispered. As far as she was concerned, as much as Becca made it look easy, she'd contained the situation. She could sashay and still guard.

The third portion of Criminal Apprehension worked with firearms. Since Sara always brought Becca to the gun range, the dog was not excited nor fearful around weapons. They were yet to test real scenarios against armed assailants.

Sara'd been a police officer for a little over five years and had already achieved the rank of sergeant. She'd seen dangerous situations get worse, but yet never needed to draw and discharge her weapon. One thing the academy trained officers to do was to serve and protect.

What they never told the public is that when a police officer shoots a suspect, right or wrong, they go on immediate administrative leave. The internal mechanism of law enforcement meant the officers were to be looked at as suspects. Essentially, Internal Affairs assess if they used their weapon in the line of duty or to commit homicide.

It wasn't like the movies. Most cops went thirty years without using their firearm against an assailant. Some rookies thought the old-timers were just fat and lazy. Sara knew better. A quick draw and happy trigger finger belonged in western movies. Taking a person's life should never be a first option; done only if necessary. She worried about gun-ho, testosterone-driven cowboys who escalated situations so they could justify homicide.

Sara was twenty-eight, lean, and well-respected. However, the locker room chatter suggested she was feisty and her bite was as bad as her bark. She didn't take shit from colleagues or the community. Being attractive sometimes put limitations on women's careers in law enforcement, but Sara combined her inherent beauty with physical attributes that not only looked good, but could kick ass, too.

Becca waited for Sara's signals for the gunfire portion. They switched volunteers. Becca scared and injured the last volunteer, so the replacement put on extra padding, anticipating Becca's fierce response.

Sara wasn't concerned about Becca's performance. She cared little about the competition. Becca was in top form, was the right age, and had mastered the proper training. Malinois as a breed, known for their physical prowess and intelligence, but Becca constantly proved herself above average in both categories. The dog's ability to grasp what Sara wanted constantly amazed her, often before Sara gave any sign. It was almost as if Becca could read her thoughts and react perfectly.

When the coordinator signaled to Sara, she remained calm, moved into the circle between the cones, and waited for the gunman to fire the blanks at the ground and start running. Becca was looking at Sara, who nodded slightly. Becca bolted the moment the suspect began shooting.

She was too fast, already five feet from the suspect, before he tossed the weapon to protect his body. He meant to turn and run, but Becca didn't run. She flew, launching from the ground, clearing nearly six feet, and sailing eight feet to collide with the volunteer. Since he barely turned to run, Becca caught the padded left arm, driving him to the ground. Sara signaled for release. Becca complied, but not before giving the poor volunteer a legitimate last tug on the arm as if saying, *I know you're playing, but if I wanted that arm, I could take it off at the shoulder.*

Again, the judges discussed something while the volunteer got help getting up. Sara watched everything from behind the sunglasses. She saw the judges. She watched the volunteer shrug out of the protective gear.

"You went through two guys," she whispered. "They don't know if they want to keep you in the competition or register you as a lethal weapon."

Becca's tail swished as she panted, leaning against Sara's side. The coordinator stepped away from the judges and approached Sara.

"Uh-oh," she whispered.

"Sergeant O'Shea, you've demonstrated your magnificent command over your K9. But the judges are as concerned as the rest of us that your partner cannot stay on the ground."

"Is that a problem?"

"Well, no, it's just that, typically, dogs run at the suspect." He glanced at Becca, almost afraid to look her in the eyes. "Your partner flew at the suspects."

Sara sighed, motioning to the field markers. "Those cones are twenty feet from me, correct?"

"Yes."

"Becca can jump ten feet from a fixed point and nearly twenty feet from a running start. She assessed the gunman's distance and figured the shortest distance between two points was in the air, not on the ground. She released when I told her. Becca performed her duty, sir."

"She *assessed*?" he asked, barely glancing at Becca.

Sara nodded and wiped her forehead. She'd applied sunblock more than a few times that day, but it was all sweated away under the pale blue sky and broiling winter sun.

The coordinator left them and returned to the judges. Sara wanted shade, water, and a shower. She knew Becca wanted ice cream, her favorite toy, and a cool bath. The entire day was fun for her, but Florida, even in February, was too damned hot.

In the last event, Handler Protection, the volunteer would pretend to physically accost Sara as Handler. People expected and understood the key word, pretend. Some dogs reacted negatively around others when they saw a potential threat. Belgian Malinois were excellent personal and family guard dogs, provided the family didn't have small children. Not that the Belgian Malinois was overly aggressive; more like if you expected a toddler to behave, the dog saw the potential to herd the toddler instead of allowing the toddler to run amok. Some people didn't understand the difference.

Several yards away, another volunteer got fitted for the final round of Criminal Apprehension. It was the *coup de grâce* event. The officers were heatedly debating it, even though she couldn't hear them. So far, Becca performed all her duties better than expected. But each preceding task was without an attacker; now a hapless volunteer would seemingly attack Sara.

"Here we go," Sara whispered. "You got me in trouble."

The coordinator approached her again. "Sergeant O'Shea, can you assure the judges that your partner will perform as expected without harming the volunteer?" he asked.

He was of average build, maybe a little soft in the middle. His crewcut hairstyle, with the regulation handlebar mustache and goatee, likely made him feel macho and superior. The cop from Lakeland seemed so cocksure. He looked like a kid pretending to be a cop instead of an actual law enforcement officer. He smiled, obviously not comprehending that if Sara sent a particular hand signal, friend or foe, Becca would castrate him faster than a veterinarian on spay and neuter day at the animal shelter.

Sara sighed, shaking her head lightly. "I'm hot, Becca's hot; I don't want to stand out here all day. Let me know if you don't want us in the last part of the competition, then say so. I'm sure my chief will talk to your chief, and everything will work itself out."

The coordinator marched away.

"He's not happy," Sara said. Becca sneezed and kept panting. She was eager to tear someone apart or play with her tennis ball; either way. It didn't matter to her.

The coordinator finished with the judges and signaled to the last volunteer to struggle into the padded shirt. They added face gear and a helmet-something the other participants didn't need. Sara didn't envy the guy in the added layers when she was in shorts, short sleeves, and combat boots. He strolled to Sara's marker.

"If your partner harms the suspect, it is an automatic disqualification."

"Isn't that the point?" Sara asked. "Isn't she supposed to protect me?"

"Just make sure you can call her off as soon as she stops the suspect."

Sara smirked. "Aw, can't she have a little fun?"

The volunteer approached the circle between the orange cones. Sara performed her routine professionally, as she did in all her training sessions. Since she stayed relaxed, Becca knew to take it easy on the subject. Sara began the pat-down search. When the suspect batted Sara's hands away, raising his right hand to strike her, Becca launched. Most dogs go for the raised arm. Becca's instincts knew that if she went for the left arm, she could pull the suspect off his feet and keep him away from Sara.

The moment she slammed into the volunteer, Becca pushed off with her powerful hind legs, throwing clawed dirt into the air like hooves on a pitch. Their suspect spun away, and Sara commanded Becca to release in midair. The jaws opened, and the suspect tumbled away. Becca hopped on her landing. She strolled back to Sara's side and leaned against her leg as she sat. The judges called time.

The team must achieve over 70% of the 340 points. Becca got 330 points. Becca received Regional Certification with 660 points out of

700 points. Sara was happy with second place; after all, this was Becca's first competition. The winning K9 team with 332 points had been competing for nine years. All the other dogs with over five competitions behind them never got that close to the top.

Second place was good enough for Sara. She bought Becca ice cream, and they checked out of the hotel room early. She skipped the obligatory banquet, packed, showered, and hit the road ahead of schedule. They drove the rented SUV, their goal Kansas City, Missouri. Sara drove up Interstate 75, watching the trees and the miles slide by and wondering if anything interesting was happening back in real winter weather.

Chapter Two

Overland Park, Kansas

Emma Caldwell worked at Goodlife Financial Bank for three years and hated every minute of every day. She wanted to be an entrepreneur, but she just couldn't bring herself to make the leap.

Her daily routine consisted of arriving within the five-to-seven-minute clock-in window at the top of the hour to qualify as "on time. "

She then spent an extra five minutes in the tiny breakroom, where she'd put away her cold-weather clothes, changed her shoes, and tried to deduce the latest smell emanating from the breakroom refrigerator.

That morning, it was Lowell Petersen's lunch from the day before. It was something with meat and spices that lingered on the Assistant Bank Manager's breath whenever he loitered near her teller station. Lowell was a nepotism-baby planted by his father, the bank owner, and never promoted above assistant because the branch didn't need further management. No one liked him, but he was never pushy. Being borderline creepy wasn't enough to get him transferred or terminated—not that either would happen.

Emma followed her routine by topping off her travel mug with breakroom coffee and caught up with the other tellers on the latest in-house gossip. Unfortunately, since it was a Saturday, gossip was light on subjects. Kathy Cooley got a manicure at the new nail shop inside the department store and complained that the manicurist smelled worse than Lowell's leftovers.

Lindsay Cameron was ready to pop. She was nine months pregnant, and her near-constant blathering consisted of how many times she needed to pee in a day, the weird dreams, and the strange cravings.

Sometimes, the way Lindsay talked about the disturbingly female-only processes seemed so alien to Emma it convinced her that reproducing was not in her future. Of course, Emma needed to *have* a relationship before she could consider pregnancy.

"Good morning, ladies," Lowell said, making a show of the flashy Audemars Piguet wristwatch he claimed his father bought him for steady rises in the branch's long-term amortized loans.

"I hope everyone is having a great day. Mrs. Cameron, I hope you are feeling great. Looks like you're due any day now."

"Overdue," Lindsay said, unconsciously rubbing her belly. It started around the same time Lowell found out she was pregnant and absently started using her surname instead of her first name as he did with the other branch associates. He must have some superstitious ideas about pregnant women.

"Dean is still in training at the Olathe branch, but he'll be back tomorrow," Lowell said in something between a complaint and a statement of fact. Emma thought he was still making excuses for Lindsay working in her overdue condition.

Dean Hines was the latest hire, scheduled to replace Lindsay once she went on maternity leave. He was young and not qualified for customer service or banking, always arriving with untucked shirts, rumpled ties, and dirty boots.

From day one, he flirted with Emma and Kathy. Always at different intervals, so as not to alert the other to his efforts. He could not be more obvious. Dean's playful banter gave Emma and Kathy something to laugh and chat about during lunch breaks, exchanging notes.

Emma wasn't interested in Dean at all. Even if she had been, inter-office romances in a bank branch of five employees were a messy prospect. They were fodder for the most interesting gossip amid the dullness of the workday. But only when you watched from the outside.

"Let's have a great day, ladies," Lowell said before tapping his black gold ring on the steel doorjamb for emphasis. "Early open day. Doors are unlocked."

"I should just go into labor today," Lindsay said as if it were a switch she could flip to get out of work. "My ankles are already five times bigger than normal."

They stepped through the door, following the tiny hallway leading to the teller stations and the lobby. The electronic doorbell chimed in the backroom ahead of them, setting up stations. Three tellers, one covering the drive-thru side, while two took up their regular spots. Emma sighed, signed into her terminal, and slid the *open* sign before putting on her best fake smile.

Bank policy prohibited customers from entering the lobby wearing helmets, ski masks, or face masks. However, because of the past pandemic protocols and lax security measures, Lowell no longer left his office to scold the bank's sole security guard, Leonard McCoy, for not following protocol. Leonard, a 63-year-old whose resemblance to the Star Trek actor caused him no end of playful teasing.

Leo, as he preferred to be called, had come into the bank's employment seven months ago from the Oak Park Mall. The change was a bit of a promotion since he made a little more per hour and got to carry a revolver. Leo, like the rest of the employees, paid little attention to customers who came into the bank bundled up.

During February's bitter weather in Kansas and Missouri, temperatures dropped below freezing with subzero wind gusts, making the wearing of heavy outerwear a necessity. It was below freezing when Emma'd left the apartment that morning, and seeing one to two early morning customers wearing hooded jackets wasn't uncommon.

Emma noticed that there were a surprising number of customers for eight o'clock on a Saturday morning. The norm on Saturdays was a trickle that began around 10 o'clock. Two came into the lobby right away, one making their way to Lindsay's window and the second to hers. The third held the door for three more, and the four initially lingered in the vestibule by the ATM. She turned from the person approaching her station to sip coffee from her travel mug. When she raised her head, she felt a shock as she looked into a reflection of her own face.

Emma was a rational person, bored with working a dead-end job before she could advance in the banking industry. She wanted something more, something exciting. Bank robberies were things of the past, action points in movies. Associates went through the obligatory training for bank robberies. Still, it would never happen in Kansas, never at a tiny place like Goodlife Financial, and certainly not on a Saturday morning when they just opened for business.

Emma had fantasized about robberies, even robbing the bank herself. Any banking associate who said they didn't was lying. But the very last thing Emma thought she'd see, the thing she'd remember the rest of her life, stood before her. When Emma stared up into her own rubberized smile from the first customer of the day, she nearly screamed at the sight. Staring back at her from underneath the gray hoodie was her *own* face. Even the barrel of the gun pointed at her didn't cause the same level of shock.

"Hey there," Emma's twin said. But it wasn't her voice; it was a man's voice. The face was pretty and serene, with a mild smile, but the hair was a wig under the red hoodie. His following phrase was as cliché as the notion of a bank robber in real life. "This is a stickup."

Lindsay screamed as her look-alike jumped over the countertop. The jumper's baby bulge carried no weight. The gun was real even if the pregnancy wasn't, and she, too, spoke in a man's tenor.

"Everyone step back from the counters, now! And get your hands up," Lindsay's doppelgänger shouted. Emma, Kathy, and Lindsay complied. Except Lindsay's hands went from stretched out to cradle her all too real swollen belly.

Emma watched the third man that had Lowell's face immediately rush into the assistant manager's office. He smashed Lowell's face with the butt of the pistol, driving him down. The force of the blow caused a starburst of blood over Lowell's face, sending him and the chair to the floor. The robber bent down to hit him several times with the pistol butt, blood splattering against the furniture, wall and floor.

Another man, whose face Emma could not see, went to Leo. After taking the guard's pistol, he ordered the older man to the ground. Leo obeyed. Kathy Cooley's alter ego climbed over the teller counter and motioned for Kathy to move from the drive-thru to the shared cashier's space. Lindsay's screams diminished into a constant whimper, dropping to her knees, backed up against the cabinets, holding her baby-bloated torso.

Protocol dictated that associates comply with robbers. But Lindsay's moaning whimpers, on the floor beside Emma, jump-started some maternal instinct Emma didn't know she possessed, and she kneeled by Lindsay. She put her arms around her. Kathy remained upright, hands up, and crying.

The fake Dean Hines strolled around the counter from the breakroom, smiling and holding a gun on the women. "Don't even think about the alarms," he said in a snarl. The robbers had missed the fact that Dean was training at another branch.

The man standing over Leo forced the old man to lie on the opposite wall from the cashier's windows. He turned, and Emma gasped at who she saw.

It was someone she never thought would be in Missouri or Kansas or ever needed to rob a bank. The action star was too famous for Oakland Park or Goodlife Financial. However, when he spoke, it was in a California accent, but lacked the surfer intonations of the characters she heard in the Wick movies or Speed, Point Break or the time travel movie with the phone booth.

"Everybody, relax. This will all be over in a few minutes," he said. His face remained unmoving, his lips sealed. He used ventriloquism to speak. "As long as Lowell does what he's supposed to do, we'll be gone in a flash." The action star looked at the bank wall clock. The CCTV camera next to the clock digitally recorded everyone who looked at it. "How are we looking, Lowell?"

Was he talking to the assistant manager or the clone?

Emma noticed the carpet growing wet under her knee. She lifted her knee, tracing the puddle back under Lindsay, who was sitting on the floor.

"Lindsay," she whispered.

"What happened?" Dean growled. "What's going on?"

Emma looked up at Dean—no, *not* Dean; it was another copy. His face didn't move when he talked.

"Her water broke."

"Aw, shit," spat the Dean lookalike.

"Yo, we've got to go," the counterfeit actor shouted in a thick California accent. "I'm working on it," Lowell's facsimile shouted from the office. His voice muffled from under the unmoving face.

Emma could see through the glass wall separating Lowell's office from the teller stations. Lowell—the real Lowell—lay on the floor, unmoving. Was he dead? There was so much blood. Did his evil twin kill him? The replica sat at the desk, using two gloved hands on the keyboard. There was a collection of devices on the desk; one plugged into the USB ports of the branch assistant manager's computer.

The robbers must understand that modern banks rarely have enough cash to be worth stealing. Most of the banks today make only electronic online transfers. Emma knew this, and it further dismissed any fantasy of robbing the place. Everyone thought it, but no one ever did it. Not until that day.

"Emma," Lindsay whispered, squeezing Emma's hand hard. Emma bent to listen to her. Lindsay gasped and panted as if she'd run a marathon. Her face showed a sheen of sweat. "The baby... the baby is coming."

Emma wanted to kick the false Dean in the kneecap. She wanted to grab his gun, shoot him, then turn and shoot the action star and her own face through the glass partition before dropping into a crouch and putting a bullet between the eyes of Lowell's double.

She would finish by putting Kathy's double in a chokehold until he passed out. But of course, these were yet more flights of fancy of Emma's mind. The whole situation felt like it was all fantasy. But, the unavoidable reality was Lindsay's baby was coming, those were real guns, and the bank robbers were real, and they were all in real trouble.

Emma looked up into her own face. The man under the mask stared at her, leveling his pistol at Lindsay. Emma did something she never thought could happen in a million years. She covered Lindsay's body with her own, shielding the baby and mother before closing her eyes.

"Something to remember me by," the actor's face roared. Emma's eyes jerked open at the sound of the gunshot. The sounds of rushing feet and someone shouting, "What the fuck did you do that for?" filled the small building. Then, in only a beat of her heart, the masked invaders were gone.

Emma tried to regain her composure, astounded she still lived. She realized she was still atop Linsay. Emma rose slowly, then helped the mother-to-be to sit up. She slowly stood up to ensure the lobby was empty when she saw Leo's body slumped against the wall, blood splatter dyeing the wall above him.

Emma turned and bit her hand to keep from screaming. She stumbled over to her desk and dialed 911 on her desk telephone. As soon as she reported the robbery, the assault, the murder, and the need for an ambulance for Lindsay, she collapsed onto the floor, sobbing uncontrollably.

Chapter Three

Kansas City, Missouri

The Kansas City Missouri Police Department (KCMPD) comprised six patrol divisions: Central, East, Metro, North, Shoal Creek, and South. Sergeant Sara O'Shea was one of three K9 officers within the department and had the most seniority. Her unit leader, Lieutenant Charlie Bertrand, headed central patrol but gave Sara special consideration regarding high-profile crimes. Becca was a distinguished and decorated officer, and he respected her and Sara.

Bertrand answered directly to Deputy Chief Ramona Cobb, a no-nonsense, no-bullshit black woman who loved the media push around Becca. Whenever she could put Becca in the spotlight, Cobb did it.

Fortunately, Sara also exhibited high-profile appeal. She manifested athletic prowess, was strong, with a striking beauty that sometimes caused suspects to say things out loud they probably shouldn't say at all. Her central heterochromia eyes accented her rectangular face. Both deep blue eyes contained a starburst of gold surrounding the pupils. She had naturally wavy honey ash-blonde hair, inherited from some Nordic ancestry, along with a subtly rounded nose.

Sara knew her smile gave away dimples, so she used it sparingly. However, regarding specific details, Sara could use her status and Becca's appeal to jump divisions and work as added details for certain crimes.

Just before noon that Saturday morning, dispatch routed a call through to Sara's phone instead of using the radio. She thumbed the hands-free mic.

"What's up?" Becca poked her head through the open partition, nuzzling Sara's neck. "Not you, silly. I was on the phone."

"Are you calling me silly, Sergeant?" Chief Cobb asked.

"No, ma'am, I was talking to my partner. What can I do for you?"

"Do you know where Goodlife Financial Bank is?"

"Isn't it on Blue Ridge Boulevard?"

"Yeah, that's it. I need you to head there ASAP for an inter-agency assist. The FBI is there. There was a bank robbery."

"Another one?"

Sara read the inter-department updates daily since the homicide at Boon Financial Holdings in February.

"Yeah, I know. They hit it this morning around ten. There's one fatality and one in hospital who's not expected to make it. The FBI wants boots on the ground doing the grunt work. They don't want to get their feet cold in those shiny black shoes," said with a dose of snark.

Sara felt a swell of excitement that Becca noticed and sniffed Sara's ear. Goosebumps rushed down her neck. "I can be there in fifteen minutes." She checked the rearview mirror before flipping the lightbar switch. She left the sirens off but did a quick U-turn in light traffic and put the pedal down.

"Listen, surprisingly, most of the press hasn't gotten wind of this yet, so there might only be a few media on site. Once word gets out, they're gonna be on this like sharks. Blood in the water, you know. You and Becca go right in. You have clearance, so don't let any tough guys stop you. Let the Special Agent in Charge know you're there and see exactly what kind of support they need." There was a shuffle of paperwork over the vehicle speakers before Cobb continued. "Um, thought I wrote the guy's name, but I can't find it."

"I'll figure it out."

"Hey, Sergeant, if Becca can solve this for the feds, it would make the department look good. I can get more funding when K9s are heroes. People love heroic dogs."

Sara ended the call before reaching back to scratch Becca under the chin, adding, "Are you a hero girl?"

The black SUVs and KCMPD vehicles cordoned several hundred yards from the bank. They closed down the corner of East 43rd Street and South Crysler Avenue. The gas station next door to the bank wasn't allowing patrons. They cut the off-ramp from US Highway 40. Regarding crime scenes, it was still fresh and spicy, just the way Sara liked it. She looked at her watch. 11:44. She looked around the scene, surprised that the only media present was a news crew from the local CBS affiliate, KCTV, the field reporter already on camera even though they yet had no facts.

"I'm looking for whoever's in charge?" she asked, approaching the first official-looking agent. Except for his shoes, he'd dressed for coat weather. Sara smirked. "I bet your feet are cold."

"Well, *now* they probably will be," he said, rolling his eyes. "What do you need, Sergeant? We've got a liaison officer in the mobile unit over there."

"Deputy Chief Cobb told me to find the Special Agent in Charge," she said, shrugging as if seeing a fatal bank robbery wasn't a big deal. "I'm here because someone here asked me to be here."

He used the smartphone from his pocket. His breath clouded his face, bouncing off the screen. He said a few words, nodded and put away the phone. She wondered if nodding during phone calls was something he did often.

"You're looking for Special Agent Nicole Sheppard," he said. "She's running the show." There was a hint of something between distrust and disdain Sara picked up. "She's in the back." He offered her something from his outerwear pocket and stomped his feet. "Put these on before you get inside."

Sara accepted the disposable booties and walked through the series of taped-off sections. Forensic teams worked inside large tents, collecting and searching for evidence. Sara's uniform allowed her access beyond all the taped-off sections right to the front doors. She gave the same speech to the next agent, who relayed the information before being granted access to the inside of the bank.

Sara glanced quickly at the body cam on her chest to ensure it was actively recording before entering the crime scene. Her pausing to put on the paper booties didn't draw attention. If the feds noticed the BWC, she'd turn it off. If they were too busy with the crime scene, the body-worn camera was an excellent way for Sara to collect evidence without even trying.

One of the two agents wearing booties and nitrile gloves barely glanced at her as they scanned for fingerprints around the ATM in the vestibule. Th other opened the door for her and the dog. The bank's interior was a large lobby with several teller stations on tall counters. To the left were three open offices with loan officer and branch manager placards on the doors. On the right were two offices, one without glass walls. The bank manager's private office sat to the left. The open door showed a pathologist inside wearing PPE coveralls, a mask, and goggles. She saw massive bloodstains on the walls and floor.

The manager's office had two doors: one accessed the lobby, the other behind the teller counters. Presumably, the restrooms and the main keycard staff entrance were down the hall to the right.

"If you have nothing to add or didn't bring us coffee, you can leave," the woman said in Sara's direction from across the lobby. She stood outside the doorway to the manager's office, watching the pathologist play with the evidence on the floor.

Sara sighed. She knew he wasn't playing, but that thought made the situation more manageable.

"Deputy Chief Cobb told me to find the Special Agent in Charge," she said, passing the lobby check stand and walking toward death's calling card.

"Alright, you found me." She lifted her palm. "That's good; now you can run along."

"I'm Sergeant O'Shea," she said, pointing to the emblem on her uniform's sleeve. "K9."

That changed everything. "Ah, alright, great, come along." The woman wore a long black coat better suited for TV detectives or warmer weather. She wore sensible shoes even if they weren't cold weather rated and black slacks with a button-down white shirt. Even if she'd not introduced herself, Sara knew immediately that she was the lead on the investigation as the woman strolled across the lobby and people moved out of her way.

Sara followed the woman past the second bloodstain and down the hallway to the right of the teller stations. They passed the restrooms and continued past two more closed doors on the left. The right wall was the windowless exterior of the bank, with cheap department store artwork adorning an otherwise cold brick façade.

She glanced at Sara's profile. She looked up slightly to find her eyeline. "What's your name again?"

"Sergeant O'Shea."

"Special Agent in Charge Nicole Sheppard," she said, but didn't offer her purple nitrile glove. Sara wore her neoprene shooting gloves, which were fine for driving in cold weather and keeping fingerprints off crime scenes. "I'm going to introduce you to my Number Two. He'll take you where I need you to take your mutt and sniff around."

Sara stopped walking, forcing Sheppard to stop and turn around.

"What are you doing? I don't have time for looky-loos."

Sara knew to count to ten before she spoke. It was a tactic that worked when dealing with drunks, chauvinists, and ignorant people. Sara was careful because she knew everything she said could come back to haunt her, especially when the body-cam caught the stultified face of the FBI agent.

"Special Agent in Charge Sheppard, I am here at the request of Deputy Chief of Police Cobb. She informed me you requested a K9 unit." Sara took a bold step forward. "I want you to understand that I do not expect and will accept no one disparaging my partner. Her name is Becca, and although she might be three years old, she has got more training hours in law enforcement than you and I put together. The University of Helsinki in Finland has determined her breed is the smartest dog breed on the planet. She can run thirty miles an hour. Her breed can jump fifteen feet and climb a twenty-foot wall. Under perfect conditions, she can detect a scent from five to ten miles. She can find drug residue on anyone inside this building, including any federal agent who's practiced recreational marijuana use. She can find bombs, lost children and an individual based on the aftershave he used a week before. Becca is a lot of things: stubborn, hard-working, alert, and energetic. She came in second this year at the USPCA Region One competition in Florida.

"Becca is not a _mutt_. Becca is a fully certified police officer, and she is my partner."

Sheppard's jaw snapped shut.

Sara knew well that her voice traveled throughout the corridor. Other agents, unseen behind doors, likely heard her. She didn't care.

"My apologies," SAC Sheppard said. "I insulted your partner."

She started walking down the hall again. At the end of the hall, Sheppard rapped on the door. It opened to a man in a black sweater, jeans, and a few weeks of whiskers on his face.

"She's all yours," Sheppard said. "Sergeant, meet my Number Two. He's the one who will coordinate the investigation and requested your involvement."

She didn't say goodbye or wait for anyone to react to the introduction before stomping stiff-legged back to the murder scene.

Sara watched Sheppard's departure, thinking about how it would show up on camera and how they would circulate the footage around the department. It might even make it to the next Christmas party video montage they showed every year at the department. Sare knew some would find the footage humorous.

"Hey there, Sergeant..." he started and leaned closer—close enough for Sara to smell his cologne, something spicy and musky.

"O'Shea," finished Sara.

He leaned against the doorjamb and smiled; hazel eyes ablaze as he watched his superior depart. "Listen, a few things before we go any further. I don't care if she considers me her Number Two, as she puts it. I don't care that we've got the blood of two dead men about thirty feet from us. Of course I care, sure, but I can't help them unless I solve this crime. I probably don't look like much, but I'm coming off working a lot of nights undercover, and I'm jetlagged because I just got reassigned this morning."

He looked at his wristwatch. "I got detailed fifteen minutes after the robbery, jumped on a plane from Virginia, and here I am. I got here about half an hour ago."

"Were you traveling by rocket? The robbery happened at ten."

"Nope, the robbery happened immediately after the branch opened. They're open from eight until noon on Saturdays. It is Saturday, right?"

Sara nodded.

"Well, we've been putting feelers out to the media, and someone tugged at the ten o'clock thread. That means we've been two hours ahead of them. That's not too shabby in the digital age."

"Alright, what do you need from me and my partner?"

"Well, the first thing I need is some breakfast and coffee. You can take me to get that."

"I'm not a chauffeur."

"No, but I am her Number Two, which means I'm her puppet, and you're my lead. I don't know this town. I'm no expert on bank robbery, but I do know criminals, and they are all idiots." He winked, actually *winked* at her. No one winked anymore. He added, "Nothing we've found so far is going to lead us to the bad guys, but something will, and if I'm going to oversee this case, I need to get some nourishment."

He reached back into the room. He grabbed and donned a jacket and motioned back down the hall. As they began walking, he leaned over and said in a small voice, "And everyone needs a good dressing down once in a while."

Was the statement referencing Sara's standoff with his SAC or something she didn't catch yet?

Sara frowned.

"So, take me to breakfast. I'll buy you lunch, and we'll get to know each other." He held up a purple-gloved hand. "In a professional capacity," he added. "Then, you and your partner can work your magic." He wiggled his fingers for emphasis. "Oh, and one more thing."

"Your name?" she asked.

"Nope, that's not important." He pointed at the body cam. "I'll be taking that video footage into evidence now," indicating her body cam. His troublemaker smile made her smile and itch at the same time.

Chapter Four

There was a sweet time between the lunch rush and dinner at the diner Sara frequented when customers were done with lunch and not moseying in for supper. She staked out a cop spot inside that faced the rest of the patrons, windows, and entrance, and put her back to a wall near the restrooms and emergency exit.

"Hey, Sara," the waitress said upon arrival. "Do you want the regular, or should I bring menus?" Claudia Bowen was the daughter of the owners. She possessed a good head on her shoulders, and the rest of her body displayed various glorious tattoos and a fondness for piercings. Claudia spoke to Sara, but the moment her eyes spotted Number Two, walking through the door, they stayed on him and his disarming smile.

"Hi," she flirted as he approached the table

"Hi," he said with a tilt of his head.

Sara had discovered the Hideaway Diner off US 40 South a couple of years before, five miles from the current crime scene. It was a little out of the way, a little outside her patrol route, and gracefully far away from the bustle of the city. They accepted Becca as a patron, never asking twice. Sara liked the place because Becca, in a booth seat, could sit without being too obvious or lie down and disappear like a predator waiting in the shadows. She was almost invisible to the diner's other customers.

"I'll have the usual," Sara said, thumbing at her new FBI friend, who sat down after having stayed behind at the car to gather his bag. "You can bring a menu for him."

"No, that's fine," the man said. "Just bring me a southwest omelet, three strips of bacon fried up crispy, biscuits and a black coffee. And keep the coffee flowing."

"Well, all right." Claudia's Kansas accent flared as she batted her eyes and swung around to ensure he noticed her attributes as she walked away.

Becca watched him, but it surprised Sara to see the FBI guy wasn't interested. He had a small travel bag that showed a lot more rough miles on it than did he.

"Um," he said, pausing before sliding further into the booth seat. Becca'd already claimed the spot, laying down, glancing from Sara to the agent, wondering if she should make room or tear his testicles off.

Sara motioned to Becca to exchange places, and the dog dutifully dipped under the table and climbed into the same booth seat as Sara. Since Becca couldn't lie down because Sara sat on the seat too, she wedged against the cushion and the wall, then settled for staring at the agent.

Sara shrugged out of her winterized jacket, hanging it on the back of the booth so it was in sight and accessible. He pulled off his jacket and tossed it on the bench next to the worn bag. He was wearing a sweater underneath.

"Feeling the cold?" she asked, pointing out the sweater.

"Hell yes," he replied. "Yesterday, it was around 30 degrees Celsius where I was. Around 102 for you Fahrenheit folks."

"Hmmm. You never told me your name," she said.

He clicked his tongue, smiling at her. "Is it because I'm mysterious?" he asked.

"Annoying would be more like it."

He laughed; a genuinely deep and pleasant sound that made the kitchen cooks dip their heads under the counter window to see him. She noticed him adjust slightly because his service piece was in a pancake holder at his back. Claudia wore a heated grin when she brought three drinks, two in glasses and one in a bowl. All three were water.

"Coffee will be up in a second. Brewing a fresh pot just for you."

Sara spread paper napkins over the placemat before placing the water bowl in front of Becca. She glanced at the agent, observing him mildly while slowly lapping at the water.

"She's incredible," he said. "You've done well with her."

"You've been around police dogs before?"

"Military. I was with an MWD in North Africa. And did a tour with another team in Afghanistan."

Military working dogs were four-legged fighters that saw more action than most soldiers out of basic training. They did more than their share of the hard work, IEDs, search and destroy, even finding hard-to-reach terrorists. It had been a Belian Malinois named Cairo with Seal Team Six when they killed Osama Bin Laden. Some military leaders saw them as disposable soldiers. Sara saw them as veterans.

"Mine was a good team. Everyone got to come home. Everyone." His eyes lingered on Becca, and Sara understood he meant the K9 units, too.

Her eyes met his for a moment. Because of the overhead table lighting, they took on a purplish hue. Odd. He removed a laptop from the travel bag, logged into the system, and turned the screen to face Sara.

"You're welcome to go through these images and reports," he said. "I don't need to remind you it's all classified, and nothing on here is available to the public. It's between me, you, and Sheppard, and Becca, of course. If it gets out, she'll claim it was KCMPD, anyway."

Sara began scanning the reports. She saw six robberies over the course of two years and noted the locations. "They're traveling east to west," she said. "They're hitting more banks at shorter frequencies."

"And they're escalating their violence."

Sara spun the laptop screen away from Claudia as she approached the table with their meals on a tray. She sat it on a nearby table and then turned to pour a large mug of steaming coffee for the agent.

"Ah, the nectar of the gods," McConnell said as he took a long sip, ignoring the heat.

"I see Becca's learning computer skills now," she said, placing matching plates in front of Sara and the agent. "So, mister, are you under arrest, or are you working with Sara?"

His smile flashed, and his eyebrow cocked. "Oh my, does she bring a lot of suspects to dine here?"

"Nope, you're the first. It's usually her and Becca and reports."

Sara only stared at the agent as he addressed Claudia. "Well, I requested Sara to help me with a case I'm working on," he said, crooked his finger at the waitress and leaned so Claudia folded at the waist to get close as he whispered loud enough for Sara to hear, "Special Agent Bruce McConnell, FBI."

"Ooh, that's exciting," Claudia said, glancing at Sara. It wasn't hard to notice the impish grin and raised eyebrows. "I'd best get back to work. Enjoy your meals."

Sara decided he didn't look like a Bruce McConnell. For that matter, he didn't look or act like an FBI agent. Her direct experience with agents typically happened during training seminars, where they wore professional masks and manners, convinced they were better than lowly police officers or sheriff's deputies.

He offered to share a small bottle of hand sanitizer, which he took from his jacket, before he rubbed his hands together and looked over the meal. His bold black eyebrows knitted.

"Where do I start?" McConnell asked.

"I don't care." Sara sat in front of a side dish of burnt ends. She offered one to Becca. The select cuts of steak were the signature of the restaurant. Becca always ate a small helping when they visited.

Sara usually ordered cheesy corn and chicken spiedini as sides, both ubiquitous in Kansas City. A side of fries always came with every order.

"You selected me, Special Agent McConnell?" she asked.

"Well, yeah, of course," he said, like it was trendy social media. "I needed someone who knew the area, and I read about you and Becca. I figured any cop would do for the lay of the land, but a K9." He glanced at Becca. She appeared more interested in the laptop screen than in their meals. "That was just icing on the cake." He shrugged, popped a piece of bacon in his mouth, and talked as he chewed. "Plus, I read a little on the plane, and you came highly recommended."

"I see," Sara said before sipping water. She couldn't figure him out. On the one hand, he was charming; on the other hand, he was borderline scruffy.

"And drop the formalities, okay? Call me Bruce. Can I call you Sara?"

"You can call me Sergeant O'Shea." Sara grinned and tossed a burnt end in the air, and Becca snatched it. She did it while watching Mc-

Connell, not the dog. Sara turned the laptop toward her again to read more.

McConnell ate and shared details she didn't directly see. "They're going after more banks with an urgency that tells me they've refined their technique. It's brilliant and becoming deadly. Before the assaults and the homicide, they were looking at five years, tops. Now, they'll get life or get dead."

"The last bank, a month ago," Sara said. "Boon Financial Holdings — that's about five miles from here. And two miles from Goodlife Financial, that's ballsy even for experienced robbers."

"I figure we've got about three weeks before they go after another bank."

"Here?"

"I believe so. It's cold. You can bet they're renting a place in the area here. Criminals tend to stay in one place when it's cold, at least until it gets too hot. They're getting good at their trade, which fits the profile."

"What about the violence?" she asked. The file included photos from the Boon Financial robbery, including the body of a teller, Joey Masters, who'd gone for the alarm.

There were also more evidence photos of victims from Goodlife, all the tellers, Lindsay Cameron, the woman who gave birth in the back of an ambulance, and the late Lowell Petersen and Leonard McCoy. Lowell had suffered a fractured cheek, broken nose, and lost two front teeth, and, more importantly, a fractured skull. He later died during surgery to stem the cranial bleeding. "That's fairly new."

"They've gotten a taste for blood, like a dog can…"

"That's a myth," Sara interrupted

"Alright, but these guys are gamers turned criminals. They're AV club geeks graduating to big-time scores. They've seen more video game violence than schoolyard fights." He sipped his water before wiping his mouth with a napkin.

"I think they're dealing with internal problems. A couple of their guys are taking it too far. He is enjoying it, and that's only gonna get worse. The others were fine with the pretending and the guns. But a couple of them didn't get enough hugs from Daddy, and now they've turned killer.

"From the witnesses, we understand the other guy killed McCoy as they were leaving the bank just because he could, shouting at the man before he shot him point blank. He's the group's psychopath. Petersen didn't need to be bludgeoned to be compliant, but his assailant took it a step further and beat him so severely he died. The psychosis may be spreading. I think with their next job, we'll have another two or more deaths. There might even be a standoff before it's over, with everyone bleeding or dying. A lot more people are going to get hurt if we can't stop them."

"What makes them look like their victims?" Sara asked. "The CCTV footage of their faces looks identical to that of the bank employees."

"Ah, yeah, I'm shocked we haven't seen that on TV yet. Excuse me."

He took back the laptop, tapped on the keys, used the touchpad, and turned it so Sara could see the 3D printing machines.

"Remember when 3D-printed guns became a problem for the TSA and ATF? What about wearing someone else's face in public to confuse the facial recognition software that's everywhere nowadays? They stake out the bank and get images of the employees, and no one would look twice at them entering the bank. Remember, all the robberies have occurred just after the banks open. Plus, you have zero chance of pinning any ID on them because the poor employees just see themselves staring back."

Sara considered the broad-reaching implications of disguising your face using someone else's, even famous people.

"So, there's no way Keanu Reeves robbed Goodlife Financial?" she smirked.

"No, we checked with his publicist. And if you followed their trends before, he was Patrick Swayze at Aegis Bank. And before that was Gary Busey. You see the simplicity?"

"No, I think a bunch of idiots have become obsessed with technology and 80s action flicks." She tossed another burnt tip to Becca. "I'm curious why you wanted a K9 for what appears to be a high-tech job. They're not stealing cash; they are grabbing online accounts. Becca's good, but unless you plan to digitize her and send her into the Matrix, she's about as stuck as I am."

McConnell laughed again, heartily and genuinely. "Maybe someday, but I believe no matter how good anyone thinks they are, they are never as good as a K9 officer."

Sara stirred at the statement. Was he trying to flirt, or did he mean it?

"Dogs are smarter and better at hunting criminals than even the forensic team. I requested you and Becca because I can find them with your help faster than computer forensics can track them."

"How are they getting into the systems?"

McConnell reached into his bag and tossed the gadget to Sara. Becca watched it, turning her head slightly, trying to make sense of it.

"That's available to the public."

"It looks like a toy." It was palm-sized, white, with orange buttons resembling those on a game console with a small LCD screen, a microSD port, and a USB-C port.

"About a hundred and seventy bucks," he said. "It can hack Wi-Fi systems. Ultra-light can scan high and low frequencies..."

"I assume it has an independent CPU?" Sara turned the device in her hand.

McConnell looked impressed. "Yes, an ARM Cortex CPU, 1024KB Flash, 256KB SRAM..."

She nodded, "And multiple input types that handle nearly every computation device. Clever little tool."

She handed it back. Sara absently noticed he didn't wear a wedding band. *That's got to help when working undercover jobs*, she thought.

"This is part of the device set they used to hack into the bank's mainframe. With the manager's access points, they can get into any user account, hit the large holders, convert the money to crypto, add that to a digital wallet anywhere in the world, and whoosh, they're gone."

"Leaving blood and now bodies behind them," Sara said, finishing his thought.

"It's a flawed system. They have loose cannons, and they're becoming lemmings with guns now. I'm afraid it'll probably get much worse before we can get to them."

"Alright, you want Becca to sniff around the bank?"

"No, I think we need to hit this from the side." He tapped a key, bringing up Lowell Petersen's image again. "See this dearly departed little shit? He's been embezzling money from Daddy's bank for years. So far, the financial forensic geeks have him on more than half a million in stolen funds he's siphoned from various accounts. They're digging deeper because it looks like he learned all his secrets from Daddy." He sipped coffee. "I want to go for a walk."

"What now?"

"No, I mean, when we're done, even later tonight... if you want. I don't care. I got carte blanch on the case and don't need to check in with Sheppard. She doesn't really want you anywhere near the bank. But after the place empties out, I'll get Becca inside.

He took another long sip of coffee and continued, "I think they're separating when they take a place. I think they're coming and going in separate cars. They can walk a mile wearing someone else's face, and no one is the wiser. I think they arrived in separate cars because six men coming out of one car look more like a clown show than a bank robbery. They probably don't even have a driver. They arrive separately, scatter when they leave, and then take off the faces, freeing them to go anywhere."

Sara gave Becca the rest of the burnt tips. Becca took her time eating, even lapping water between nibbles. Sara liked his trajectory. He worked out a theory that needed empirical evidence.

"You think she can find a trace of them even in the cold and after all this time?" McConnell asked.

"Oh yeah, if Becca gets a scent, she can track it."

"We'll hang back for a while," he said, leaning against the cushion. He'd finished eating but hadn't finished his plate, telling more about his habits than she would get directly from him. Sara always got a to-go container and a follow-up of burnt tips helping for Becca later. They got two to-go boxes for later. "Do you have to be somewhere? A boyfriend? Husband? I'll authorize the OT through my channels."

Sara gave him half a smirk, so the dimples didn't give away the answers to the camouflaged questions. "Nope, I'm free to help." She hadn't meant to make it sound so official. She looked at Becca, hoping to hide the light blush she felt.

McConnell's forehead wrinkled with a deepening frown as he said, "You know I can't tag you as an O'Shea; you don't strike me as one.

I'm not knocking being Irish, my you. I've met plenty of Irish cops in my line of work."

Sara smiled, wondering if he knew already and wanted to see if she admitted it, or if he genuinely asked for the sake of conversation.

"It's my married name," she said. "I kept the name and dropped the husband."

"Oh." He leaned back, head tilting lightly. It was the same motion Becca used when she saw a squirrel, speculating if it was a furry drug dealer in disguise or something she could chew on. "Oh, I see." He nodded in acceptance.

"My maiden name is Young," she said, not sure why she'd offered it so willingly.

If he had more questions about surnames and ex-husbands, McConnell swallowed them with a sip of coffee. He motioned to Claudia to refill the mug and segued into another embarrassing subject.

"You got a little sun in Florida, I see," he said, motioning to his cheeks and nose. "It brings out your freckles."

Sara didn't know if she wanted to slap him or smile at him. He was charming and irritating all at once.

"How did you know I was in Florida?" She pretended to rub her nose with the back of her hand to hide the smile.

"I told you I did some reading on the plane."

"And you're jetlagged?"

"Yup, I came up from South America," he said, grinning lightly. "There's some G14 classified shit down there."

Claudia sashayed over and refilled the mug.

"Thanks," he said with a bright smile.

With an undisguised emphasis she replied, "My pleasure," and walked away.

"Why aren't you still down there?" She'd noticed the bronze tone of his skin, even on the backs of his hands up his arms, when he pushed the sweater sleeves back. There were hints of tattoos on his forearms, but she forced herself to focus. "Your boss doesn't seem to like you. If someone other than Jean-Luc Picard called me Number Two, I'd shoot them."

"You have shot no one in the line of duty *yet*."

He winked again.

Damn it.

"Sheppard doesn't like how I got reassigned. She took the high road to get in charge; she thinks I took the low road. When you go undercover, you get special considerations after your time's done." He laced his fingers behind his head as he faced her, giving Sara a better idea about his broad shoulders, defined biceps, and a few more hints at the tattoos—maybe tribal, maybe Celtic.

"Sheppard got me dropped on her as soon as she got assigned to the robbery. I never did robbery and was looking for something a little more practical than running from drug dealers." He looked at Becca. Behind those eyes existed a prolonged sadness.

"I chose here, and here I am."

"You chose to come *here*?"

"You want to know what's funny about that? I didn't know there was an active case before I got the posting. A map of the US was on the wall. Though I wanted to go somewhere I hadn't been before, somewhere that wouldn't get noticed. I threw a dart."

"You hit Kansas City?"

"Actually, I hit outside Harrisonville, Missouri, but the FBI doesn't have a field office there. So, you got me."

Sara wondered about the agent's carefree attitude. Was that a benefit or a risk?

McConnell used the hand sanitizer again, offering it to Sara before slapping his hands together and rubbing vigorously. "What do you say, Sergeant O'Shea? Do you want to go hunting with Becca and find some bad guys?"

She used the sanitizer and put it on the table between them. Sara called Claudia over for two to-go boxes. While Claudia got the check and the containers, Sara relented. "Yup, let's go hunting."

He took another big swig of hot coffee. She put her hand on Becca's bulletproof vest. "And you can call me Sara. By the way, make sure you wear something warm. It's going to snow later."

Chapter Five

They planned to meet after midnight. Given that the bank was a crime scene until otherwise designated, the FBI monitored the location using recruit agents, who were cutting their teeth on the very real boring aspect of their chosen profession.

Sara deposited Special Agent Bruce McConnell at Goodlife Financial, exchanged phone numbers, and returned to the Central Patrol Division Station. She checked in with the watch commander and parked at her desk while Becca patrolled the interior of the cop shop before settling in her spot, an elevated canvas hammock designed for dogs. The setup allowed Becca a relatively unobstructed view of the bullpen.

Sara sent a series of emails to Deputy Chief Ramona Cobb and Lieutenant Charlie Bertrand and cc'd Commander Lewis Powell. She wanted full transparency with her superiors and to enlighten them on some aspects of crime details she felt wouldn't violate the chain of custody evidence or create rumors that might leak to social media.

She and Becca went back to her tiny single-family rental house on North Broadway, fifteen minutes from the Central Station. Listed as a bungalow, it was a little bigger than a shoebox and just enough space for her, Becca, her duty equipment, and private parking for her shop vehicle. The owners liked the idea of renting the space to a cop. Having a police vehicle in the parking space overnight kept porch pirates and mailbox bandits away.

Sara and Becca patrolled the neighborhood almost daily for Becca's run and sometimes ventured down to Penguin Park. Giant animal sculptures coated in pigeon and dove droppings didn't faze Becca because she deemed them and the children on the playground non-edible and not worth a second look.

There wasn't time for a nap before she met McConnell at the bank. With time to kill, Sara gave Becca her meal and vitamins. Sara took a shower.

The assignment wasn't anything special, just an agency assist that kept the local and federal law enforcement holding hands, so to speak.

When she picked out her after-hours outfit. She never sacrificed warmth for fashion. She'd suffered through cases in subzero temperatures for hours. Frostbite was never becoming. Becca got a pair of high-performance K9 boots designed for traction and warmth. They doubled as sandals on hot summer days if Becca spent any time on asphalt.

"What?" Sara asked, seeing Becca watch her in the bathroom mirror. She knew she'd been looking at her reflection longer than usual because the freckles and tan lines from the Florida sunglasses did show under the right light. "I know. It's stupid. But you're a girl, and well, sometimes you just want to look your best."

Becca cuffed as if agreeing.

Sara sighed, tied her hair up at the back, and wore a navy watch cap with the KCMPD logo. She put on cold-weather gear just before midnight, and they left the bungalow. The sky over the neighborhood gave off a yellow milky glow from the streetlamps. Over time, the cloud ceiling thickened and dropped. While Sara drove to the bank, a few floating snowflakes smashed against the windshield, leaving a heavy splotch of wetness to mark their demise.

"I see you brought coffee," she said when McConnell got out of the passenger side of the unmarked black SUV that idled in the outer parking lot adjacent to the bank lot. The driver glanced at Sara and Becca briefly before driving away once he'd deposited his passenger.

McConnell carried a cardboard tray and a paper bag with the local donut shop stamp. He wore cold-weather outerwear, including good boots. Clean-shaven and presumably washed and combed, his thick, wavy locks were now tucked away under the ski cap. His prominent jaw no longer hid under the whiskers. He appeared like a face for a poster promoting careers in the Federal Bureau of Investigation.

"You must drink a lot of coffee," she said, noting the four disposable travel cups on the tray.

Cloudy breath puffed from his nose and mouth when he laughed, shaking his head. "Will the coffee scent bother Becca?" he asked. "The bag isn't for us."

McConnell carried the tray and the bag to another dark SUV parked several yards from the crime scene. She wondered what kind of guy considered the K9's olfactory sense over the people's preference. Most cops didn't think twice about Becca's comfort. Outside the station, they smoked cigarettes or vaped, but no one drove Sara's shop vehicle, so she didn't worry about lingering tobacco or chemical odors.

"Every crime scene has its set of smells," she said. "Becca will figure out which ones are important to her."

Becca stood, touching Sara's leg, sniffing the air lightly before sneezing the scent of hot coffee and greasy donuts out of her sinuses. McConnell handed the junior agents the fresh coffee and snacks for the overnight stakeout. Cleared of the supplies, he returned the extra coffee cup to Sara. She ignored the young recruits in the SUV, watching her through that keen lens men used when they surreptitiously watched beautiful women. Sara was used to the side-eye glances.

They stood momentarily outside the taped barrier. Sara sipped the coffee, lightly creamed and lightly sugared. She suspected he had prepared each of the cups identically, leaning to his preference. She waited for him to make the next move. But he only appeared heavily caffeinated, clean, and scrubbed, watching Sara over the brim of his cup lip.

"So, are we waiting for someone else?" she asked in the awkward silence that only the other side of midnight brought to Kansas City.

On Sunday, many of the local shops were closed, observing the heavily influenced religious portions of the city. In Middle America, the Bible Belt stretched far enough to tighten around a metropolitan area of half a million people. This would be to their benefit because foot traffic on the streets would be minimal.

"Um, no, I was waiting for you," he said, grinning. "Sorry. Come on."

He led Sara and Becca to the bank doors. She expected them to be locked, but McConnell opened one as if it were still banking hours. The inside lights shone brightly behind the barricade tarpaulin covering the window fronts. He held the door for Sara. Becca waited outside, watching. Her brown eyes inside the black mask were onyx in the vestibule lighting.

"She doesn't like anyone walking behind her," Sara said, trading places so they could follow McConnell inside.

He lingered at the check counter, where the FBI had placed several tackle boxes set up with fingerprinting equipment and unused evidence bags.

"Do I need booties?" she asked.

"No, I see Becca's got her slippers. The forensic geeks cleared the scene. We're good." He stifled a yawn with the back of his hand. Maybe he wasn't as hopped up on caffeine as she first thought. "It's all yours."

Sara kneeled in front of Becca. She played with Becca's neck and ears. With one hand, she reached behind her back. Becca wore her bulletproof vest. Sara exchanged her uniform for an off-duty holster and a hip pouch. Becca was savvy to the one-handed gesture, and her eyes lit up, her ears melted, and her tail thumped, anticipating the next surprise.

Sara special-ordered the canvas sock monkey from an online maker. It was about nine inches long with a head topped with white fur and decorated with a smile that Sara thought made it look creepy. Its brown body comprised two arms, two legs and an oddly long tail. Becca's preference for her tools of the trade ran deep. The sock monkey was by far the best weapon in her arsenal. Sara showed it to Becca, and got bent ears, a cocked head, another sneeze, and an energetic tail wagging that wiggled the dog's butt too in reply.

"Alright, go get them."

Becca spun lightly, orienting herself before she bolted for the dead bank manager's office.

"She's not going to lick up that old blood, is she?" McConnell's face twitched between curious and sickened.

"Nope," Sara said, setting the durable sock monkey on the countertop to retrieve her coffee again. "Becca's not into junk food." She hid her smirk behind the coffee cup.

McConnell watched Becca weaving around the desk, sniffing every inch of the office. She left the office and rushed out of sight to another part of the bank. Her nails clicked on the tile floor in the breakroom and behind the teller counters. As he watched for Becca, Sara studied his striking profile.

"Is it magic?" he asked. It sounded like an authentic question.

"Is what magic?"

"Your bond with her," he said. "The way she looks at you, I almost expect her to start talking."

"She wouldn't have much to say except complain that she doesn't run enough, she's not outside enough, she doesn't go for enough rides in the rig." Sara shrugged. "I feel the same way. So, I already know what she'd say."

"What happens next?"

"If she gets something lingering, different from the layers of sameness throughout the place, Becca will return. She'll let me know she's found something interesting, something worth further investigation."

"She'll detect the bad guys?"

"And you and the rest of the agents who were in and out of this place all day. But you're hoping for a miracle. I'm thinking we might get to go for a walk outside that will probably end somewhere around the block and right back here."

"You sound doubtful."

"Oh, no, not at all," Sara said, stiffening. "I trust her with my life. But everyone has limitations, even dogs."

"What about Mr. Monkey there?"

Sara took the sock monkey from the counter. "She likes it. She'll take it with her on the walk. If she picks up a familiar scent tonight, she'll drop the monkey. Who knows, we might get lucky." Sara wondered if her face reddened with the unintentional double entendre.

McConnell wanted to ask more questions, but Becca ran past them and into the rooms to the right and back into the cashier area.

She plodded back to them and looked into Sara's eyes, dog language for affection. Then, she sat and looked at the monkey mocking her from the edge of the counter like a mischievous elf on a shelf.

Sara took the monkey and tossed it to the eagerly awaiting dog, who jumped up and snatched it from the air, pausing a moment to shake it back and forth as if it were some recently caught prey.

"Well, it looks like we're going outside again." She zipped her coat before putting on her gloves again.

"We can leave our coffees," McConnell said, taking advantage of the evidence kit. He removed items from the tackle boxes, slipping them into his heavy winter coat.

Sara opened the door for McConnell, Becca, and herself. Becca carried Mr. Monkey and quickly picked up a scent just outside the vestibule. She dropped the monkey and turned on the forensic factory in her brain and nose.

Her olfactory recess contained a maze of conical passages that increased the sensory cell surface. Danish anatomist Ludvig Levin Jacobson discovered a paired structure in the nasal sac of a human cadaver purchased from resurrectionists in 1811. Neither the body snatchers nor the deceased cared. As he removed and examined each tissue, the good doctor began labeling the organ.

Later called the vomeronasal organ, the nasal computer in canines can detect pheromones. Once detected and analyzed, a dog's nostrils move around, pinpointing the direction of scent. The moist nose also uses air currents containing trace elements of selected scents.

"Interesting," Sara said. She'd been skeptical because of the fourteen-hour delay since the crime and the amount of foot traffic. However, Becca found something she wanted to investigate. Sara took up the sock monkey, and Becca launched away.

"Is she going to run into traffic?" McConnell asked quickly.

"No, she knows to look both ways before crossing the road."

They followed her at a distance. She moved around the lot, sniffing the air and the ground. Suddenly she bolted down the hill and disappeared. Sara and McConnell followed her, trotting down the steep embankment, Becca suddenly appeared again, running toward the open, empty parking lot near the outlet mall behind the bank, they could easily see Becca rushing, zigzagging, losing, and picking up the scent again.

"Have you been with her long?" McConnell asked

"Three years. After my FTO, I went back to K9 obedience school, and there she was, just a pup. The instructors paired us and have been partners ever since."

The field training operation allowed officers to undergo probationary, observed training for six months to a year so they could become proficient independently.

"Becca was the smallest of a litter of four, and we got teamed up shortly after they weaned her."

"You're very lucky."

"You can adopt a dog at any shelter... you know that, right? They can even get shelter dogs in top form for drug trafficking, guns, and explosives."

"If I get a dog, it will be for me, not work."

"Oh," Sara giggled. "She's not working," Sara said, gesturing to the four-legged silhouette tracking invisible rabbits under the parking lot lighting. "She's having fun. We don't use negative techniques. Everything in K9 training is positive reinforcement. Becca sees crime scenes as a playground where she can choose any thread to follow."

Sara watched Becca reach the sidewalk along the closed storefronts. Most of the businesses went dark overnight, cutting unnecessary overhead costs. Becca nearly disappeared in the shadows of the awnings.

"I imagine her world as a color wheel."

"Um, I thought dogs were color blind."

"Not really. They just see different colors, different wavelengths, but mainly Becca sees with her nose. Something in her brain chooses a scent. I pretend it's a color trail, a vapor trail like riding on air currents, and she'll track it until it completely dissipates."

When they reached the storefront walkway, Becca sat panting and waiting, glancing at Sara and the monkey in her hand. Then she turned and continued onward toward the far end of the outlet mall.

"I like that image," McConnell said quietly.

She hadn't noticed him shoulder to shoulder with her until the sidewalk. Their strides quickened as Becca neared the department store corner. Becca looked back and saw Sara's hand signal for her to wait until they caught up, and again Becca sat. Once they caught up, Sara simply moved the fingers of her left hand as if she were brushing invisible crumbs from an invisible table, and the dog was off again.

At the end of the building, away from the streetlights, the paved roadway alongside the warehouse-sized concrete commerce center gave way to a grassy drop-off leading down to a polluted, frozen stream. Sara and McConnell used their LED flashlights to show the way as Becca crossed and they followed.

McConnell slipped on the ice and fell, but caught himself with his hands. Sara stopped and helped him back onto his feet. "Nice job," she teased. "You didn't even get your clothes dirty."

When they exited the ditch, they watched the dog follow a route behind the outlet mall designed for deliveries.

Broken glass glinted like diamond facets on the asphalt, and Sara breathed a sigh of relief that Becca wore her winter boots.

The lot seemed abandoned, sparsely choked with patches of dying grass amid the fallen snow. The dog sped up. As they proceeded further up the minor road behind the stores, towards the loading dock of an abandoned warehouse, the cacophony of the overgrown empty lot seemed to grow. Debris, with tangles of sedges, sickly sapling suckers, and winter-dry grass, was everywhere. Ragged plastic packaging and bags clung to the sticks and places where walls met the ground like concrete drift nets snagging human refuse after it had blown around the lots. With the wall blocking it, the breeze dropped, and Becca stopped, looking down and sniffing the ground gingerly.

"She's found something."

Sara pulled the monkey from her hip pouch and continued to the dog. By the time they reached Becca, she was already lying on the gravel and bottle cap-strewn pavement, signaling she had indeed found something of interest. She waited for Sara to step forward and investigate.

"Good job, Becca," Sara said as she tossed the monkey away from whatever had caught Becca's attention. The dog leaped after her reward.

"Well, hello there," McConnell said as he bent down to look at what the dog had found. His grinning teeth sparkled when Sara saw his face in the flashlight wash.

He handed Sara the evidence bag and plastic tweezers. "It's Becca's find; you get the honors." She exchanged her flashlight for the tools.

"That's just dumb luck," she said, glancing at Becca's smug snout with a grin.

McConnell used his smartphone to photo-document the item before collection. The material was artificial, flesh-toned, and no bigger than a half-dollar coin. Sara pinched it with the tweezers, lifting it from under the piece of gravel that pinned it to the ground. The malleable material flapped in the light breeze and drifted out of the tweezers.

It fluttered to the pavement, embarrassing Sara for not getting a better grip on it. She carefully pinned it again and slowly placed it into the evidence bag, leaving the tweezers poking out through the open flap. She handed it back to McConnell.

He folded the bag above the sample, pocketed the silicone rubber and tweezers and then began looking over a broader area. Sara's second flashlight lit up a significant portion of the ground, and she pointed at the mild scuff of blackish discoloration and area void of gravel on the pavement.

"The driver accelerated here. He must have removed the mask when he got into the vehicle. The piece tore off, and if he hadn't gunned the gas, he might not have trapped that piece under the pebble."

Sara imagined a phantom car parked behind the loading dock. She saw the driver and possibly a passenger or two climbing in and tearing off. She used the flashlight to scan the roof line, searching for CCTV cameras, and she saw a few steel stalks, beheaded of electronics, either from vandalism or targeted gunfire from years back.

The trio made their way back to the bank. This time, no one slipped on the ice.

"Damned fine detective work, Becca," McConnell said. He pulled the smartphone from his pocket. As he dialed and waited, he spoke to Sara. "I'll have a team come back here and look for more trace evidence. They'll suit up and go into that briar patch." He flashed the light over the tangle of weeds and detritus. When he spoke again, it was on the phone. "Good morning. Yeah, I know what time it is. Any time after midnight *is* in the morning. Don't you know that?"

He pulled the smartphone away from his ear so the person on the other end could shout at empty space. He winked again, but Sara kept her lips from curling into a smile.

"Alright, I get it. You're tired. I can log this evidence myself. I'll keep you up to date on the findings." He ended the call. "She'll call back."

"We can go, eh... May I?" Sara asked, reaching for his right sleeve. She used the utility belt knife to cut off the coat price tag he'd forgotten after his purchase. She handed it to him. "You're on the case."

"Sure you don't want to stick around the rest of the night? I've already been twenty-hours with no sleep. When the rainbow unicorns pour out of my hallucinations, maybe you or Becca can round them up."

"I've got patrol in a few hours. I'll get some sleep for both of us."

"Can I touch her?" McConnell asked. He kept the smartphone at the ready.

"It's up to Becca." Sara jutted her chin at McConnell. Becca glanced in his direction, sized him up, and deemed him not worth chewing up but worth a sniff.

He let her test the back of his glove before he petted her head. The smartphone vibrated in his grip. McConnell smiled and waved before turning from Sara to talk to his SAC.

"Good morning, boss, guess what the K9 just found." Tit for tat was a great way to poke a sleeping bear with no real effort.

Sara smiled as she strolled back to the patrol rig. She grabbed Becca's sock monkey's tail and played tug-of-war with her. On the way home, cornflake-sized snowflakes buffeted the windshield. Sara opened the passenger window so Becca could snap at them.

Chapter Six

Bruce McConnell drove his rented Tahoe to the new headquarters office at 11180 NW Prairie View Road, next to Kansas City International Airport.

Once inside, he carried the rubber sample in the evidence bag and headed to the office of SAC Shepperd to request expedition of the materials to Quantico Labs in Virginia.

The meeting with Shepperd was quick. He did not have to convince her that time was their enemy in this case. He went downstairs to the Evidence Custodian's office, where he presented the priority permission Sheppard had given him and filled out an FD-192 Chain of Custody form before turning the bag over to Lewis Perez, the office's Evidence Custodian.

Lewis accepted the bag from McConnell, saying, "You're the new guy working the bank robberies?"

"Yep," replied the agent. "Bruce McConnell."

"You TDA or will we be seeing you around these parts for a while?"

"For now, at least, this is permanent."

"Well, it's nice to meet you. I am Lewis... Lewis Perez. I'll make sure this is on the flight to Quantico this afternoon."

"Thanks, Lewis." Bruce turned and headed back up the stairs to his assigned cubicle. He thought about the next steps as he walked, but knew the case was now in the hands of the Quantico scientists.

Downstairs, Perez entered the information from the bag into the FBI Sentinel System, assigning a unique evidence number, taking a photo of the evidence that is digitally attached to the Chain of Custody file and the Sentinel file. He then counter signs to priority request and places the items in a large tamper-proof priority transit envelope, labeling it with the evidence number, agent name and destination.

Perez placed the envelope into the transit box to be transported to the Quantico plane early this afternoon. Once all evidence from the region bound for the FBI labs was turned in, he would lock the box and secure it with a wire and seal.

At about 12:30, Benny Nguyen, a contracted courier, stepped up to the door to be buzzed in. Perez hit the button, and the door silently opened.

"Got something for the airport?" the young man asked.

"Just one box," Perez answered as he pressed to device used to tighten the seal he'd slipped the wire into. "All set."

Benny took the box and said, "This is light."

"Yeah, just a few items today."

Benny carried the box back out the secure door, down the hall and into the loading dock area, then loaded the box into the van's cargo area, locking it in.

As he crawled behind the steering wheel, he played the same game as always, guessing the box's contents. He would never know, of course, but it was still something to pass the time.

As he drove to Wheeler Downtown Airport to turn over the box to the pilot flying to Quantico at 4pm, Benny was still playing his mental guessing game. He stopped guessing when he realized that a cacophony of brake lights in front of him had suddenly formed a wave headed his way.

The traffic on I29 stood halted ahead. He checked his watch. 3:05. The drive only takes 20 minutes on a good day, so he should be fine.

However, as the traffic crawled southward, his confidence waned. Of the 55 minutes he had, 13 had ticked away, and he had moved only about half a mile.

He got on the radio and to the hangar office that serviced the FBI. His supervisor answered the call.

"Eddie, I am stuck in traffic on I29. Do you have any idea what's going on?"

"Yes. There is a multi-car accident on the 169, just past I29. You gonna make flight time?" Eddie asked.

"Shit. I don't know. Traffic is really creeping."

"I'll see if she'll hold the flight."

Benny grew impatient as the traffic continued to crawl. Just as he reached a boiling point, the traffic picked up speed, and it started to snow.

As he merged onto Highway 169, he saw the wrecks on the side of the road. He knew there were people who would not make it out alive, and he felt remorse for the things he'd said to himself while snarled. However, he couldn't slow down to grieve. It was 3:52.

Benny drove over the speed limit and hoped that the accident had tied up all the cops. He banked off to the right on the Broadway exit and merged onto Richards Street.

He turned right at the seventh entrance to the small municipal airport and around the hangar, sliding a little to the left because of the wet pavement. The Pilatus Aircraft PC-12 NGX was sitting in front of the hangar like it was ready to roll. Benny glanced at his watch. 4:03. Three minutes behind schedule. Not bad, considering.

He jumped out of the driver's seat and ran to the back of the van. Unlocking and opening the door, he hauled the box out and, without shutting the door, ran to the cargo hatch on the left side tail section.

Constance Addler, the plane's pilot, yelled at him to put the box in the back of the passenger cabin. She was saving time by having him put inside.

Benny ran past a none too happy Constance and up the short ladder. A stout, balding man filled one of the front passenger seats. The scowl on his face caused Benny to wonder if he'd pissed everyone off.

He made the way back to the last row and tucked the container into a slot in the floor and strapped it in place. As he turned to leave, he could see Constance climbing into her seat in the cockpit. The flight's co-pilot waited to shut the door. She was a truly stunning redhead named Terri Green.

Benny stumbled on, "Have a pleasant flight," and left the plane.

By the time he walked around to close the van's rear door, the plane's prop was spinning up to speed and the plane was taxiing toward the runway. With the wind from the prop buffeting him, he went into the office.

"If you'd been a minute later, she'd have left with the cargo," said his supervisor.

"I don't control the traffic, Eddie," came Benny's retort.

"She's carrying a VIP salesperson to a meeting at Quantico. That's why she was getting impatient."

"Yeah, she's also probably trying to outrun the snowstorm. It's really beginning to come down, and from the looks of those clouds, it's going gonna get bad."

"Damn. I was hoping to make up a little time, but this weather is getting rough," Constance said to Terri.

"Maybe we can get above it."

"I think the ceiling is too high," Constance replied. "We're just gonna have to tough it out."

"Can we at least get above the precipitation?" Terri asked.

"We can see," came the reply as Constance pulled back on the yoke and the plane assented.

After a couple of minutes, the moisture falling on the windscreen lessened, although the jostling of the plane did not.

"That's a little better than before," Terri said.

The flight from Kansas City to Quantico normally took between two and two-and-a-half hours, but the storm might throw this off slightly.

Their passenger, Mr. Stanley Ferentz, Head of Development for Agilent Technologies, makers of the FBI's GC-MS systems, was on his tablet prepping for his meeting the next day.

The PA clicked on, and he heard the pilot say, "We are in for a bit of turbulence this afternoon, so please keep your seatbelt fastened and minimize moving about in the cabin. Looks like we will be out of the soup somewhere near the Indiana and Ohio border. I will keep you updated."

Ferentz hoped the female pilot knew what she was doing as he fastened his seatbelt. Just as he heard the click of the fastener, the plane dropped momentarily, and the cabin became weightless. Ferentz grabbed his tablet, and then gravity returned. "Sonuvabitch," he muttered under his breath. He should have flown commercial.

The plane jostled for the next 95 minutes until it burst through the wall of the storm and suddenly they were in smooth and partly cloudy skies.

Constance and Terri both sighed a breath of relief and relaxed a bit. Each of the women took turns using the plane's small restroom.

Before taking her co-pilot's seat again, Terri said, "Let me see if our guest would like a snack," as she prepared to become the flight's attendant. "You like something to drink?"

"A coffee would be lovely, thanks," smiled Constance.

Terri left the cockpit and approached Ferentz. "I think it will be smooth the rest of the way, sir. Would you like a drink and a snack?"

"How much longer until we land?"

"I suspect about an hour, maybe sooner if we catch a good tailwind. Drink?"

"Yeah, a diet cola and some pretzels."

"Coming right up." Terri moved to the cabinet that served as a galley on the PC-12. It held an assortment of chips and energy bars with a small selection of chilled drinks. Terri had also brought aboard a thermos that kept coffee hot for a couple of hours.

Terri retrieved Ferentz's items and gave them to him. She returned to the cabinet, poured Constance a steaming cup and grabbed a diet lemon-lime drink for herself. She held the soda under her arm and opened the cockpit door.

"I hope it's still hot enough," she said while handing the cup of coffee to the pilot.

"It'll be fine. How's the passenger?"

"He fine. Usual questions, but he will be okay until we're on the ground."

Terri took her seat and took the controls while Constance stretched and enjoyed her coffee.

The rest of the flight was uneventful, and the two women chitchatted until they were approaching Quantico.

"MCAS, this is FBI 824 requesting landing instructions," Constance radioed the tower at the Marine Corps Air Station.

Constance banked the plane to the right, making a long arch to line up with the assigned runway. The landing was smooth as silk. The plane taxied to the assigned hangar, where a car and a van sat waiting.

Terri left the cockpit and opened the exit door, barely completing lowering the steps before Ferentz was moving down them and heading to the car.

"Excuse me, Mr. Ferentz," Terri called, "Won't you need your luggage?"

Terri heard a mumbled "shit" before the man turned. Terri moved to the cargo hold, unlatched and opened the door and retrieved the small suitcase. The man snatched it from her and walked away without a word of thanks.

Terri contained herself and merely shook her head.

Bill Hickman, the contracted courier, left his van and moved toward the plane.

"Hi, Terri," he called, waving.

"Hey Bill. How are you?"

"Good. How was the flight?"

"Pretty rough. Big snowstorm over KC."

Constance joined them and said to Bill, "Your package is in the back of the cabin, not cargo."

"Okay," Bill said as he moved to the plane, then up the stairs and into the cabin. Secured behind the last seat, the package sat. He retrieved it and left the plane. "Do you want the outgoing box for Chicago in the cabin or cargo?" Bill asked after he loaded the KC box and removed the outgoing one.

"You can put it in the cargo hold," came Constance's reply.

"You got it." Bill moved to the right side of the plane. He put the small box through the open door and strapped it down, then closed and re-latched the compartment's door.

"May see you tomorrow, ladies. Josey got the flu, and we're all pulling extra shifts. Have a pleasant flight."

The plane would only be on the ground long enough to refuel and for the women to stretch their legs and grab a little dinner at the small diner that served the aircrews.

The women said goodbye, and Bill loaded the package in the back of the van.

He then drove up Russell Road from MCAS to the FBI buildings and the labs awaiting his priority package.

Chapter Seven

Bill Russell checked in the evidence box at the Evidence Control Center just inside the cargo entrance. Derek Hobarth, the duty control officer, logged in the box, broke the seal, opened it and examined each envelope to ensure the seals of each remained unbroken. He then logged each item into the Laboratory Management System (LIMS) which assigns each case a new number and prints a label, which Derek adhered to each evidence envelope. Derek took a digital picture of the envelope, which is automatically entered into LIMS, connecting it as the beginning of a collection of documents and photos that were collected to the file on its route through the building. He signed the Chain of Custody (COC) document and broke the seal on the KC evidence. He added digital photos of the contents, replaced the sample, then placed the envelope into a tray designating its priority.

In short order, Intern tech Lisa Aziz picks up all the expedited evidence and delivers each all to the Laboratory Triage Unit. There, Basma Hamadani organizes them by laboratory and determines order in cases of conflicting needs. Lisa then carries the KMC envelope to Trace Elements.

Sophie Carter took the envelopes from Lisa. She determines the order of processing, with the KC envelope third. About an hour later, she signs the COC document, and enters digital photos of the evidence and documentation of the envelope's contents.

She takes the small sample of silicone rubber from McConnell's original bag and places it under the microscope looking for any hair, fibers or particulates. Only microscopic dirt and gravel that had adhered to the sample were visible.

Sophie then turns the piece over with a pair of tweezers and examines the backside, looking for anything like striation marks that might help identify the printer used to create the mask, noting her findings. She then determines the printer settings as 0.05 mm and the type of printer used as evidenced by the patterns on the sample. Her conclusion is that the printer is a medical printer using Masked Stereolithography (MSLA). She runs a comparison through the database of 3D printers and determines it to be most likely a Formlabs, which manufactures only one MSLA printer matching all the criteria, the Form 4BL.

She enters all her observations and conclusions into LIMS and then, because of the case's priority, hand-walks the repackaged sample and hands it Johnn Van Burton in the Latent Prints lab.

Johnn signs the COC and then carefully extracts the sample from the envelope and performs a cyanoacrylate fuming test. This reveals a small portion of a fingerprint on one edge. To no surprise, the print is too small, and he cannot get a hit in the Automated Fingerprint Identification System (AFIS) database.

He enters all his observations and results into LIMS. Following Basma's instructions, he carefully bisects the sample and puts each in its own bag and envelope. He notes the action in ILMS, which generates a new COC and tracking numbers for each sample.

Like Sophie, he hand-walks the two envelopes to both Ernie Mac-Mackins of the Chemical Lab and Dr. Rose-Marie Turner in the DNA Lab.

Ernie takes the sample and uses a spectrometer to determine the chemical composition. He uses the results to determine both the formulation of the resin and silicone rubber used. Running the results through the database of manufactured goods, he can make an exact match for the resin. ANYCUBIC Water-Wash 2.0 10KG 3D Printer Resin, a very common brand. His analysis shows the composition of the mask is of a tin-cure silicone rubber with calcium carbonate fillers, consistent with mass-produced costume or prosthetic masks manufactured in Asia. Both items are readily available on the website of the Chinese company, AliExpress.

He enters all the data into LIMS and files the envelope with the other examined evidence envelopes to be cataloged and stored.

Rose-Marie first swabs the inside of her portion of the sample for any epithelial cells. The process is meticulous. Because of the size of the sample, Rose-Marie used only 2 moistened cotton swabs, applying firm rotating pressure. She places each swab in a sterile tube, labeled including case number, evidence item number, presumed swabbed location (in this case, cheek), and date and technician initials. She then begins the process for extraction setup, including cutting the swab tips into an extraction tube, adding lysis buffer to break down cell membranes and proteinase K enzyme to digest proteins. Shew then incubates the tubes at 133 F for 2 hours in a heating block with occasional vortexing to mix thoroughly.

The next day, the process of organic separation begins. Adding additional chemicals, such as a phenol-chloroform solution. She places the sample in a high-speed centrifuge to separate the DNA into an aqueous layer, which is carefully removed. The DNA is now separate from the other elements.

Her next steps are the DNA precipitation, adding cold ethanol and sodium acetate to force the DNA to precipitate out of solution. A run in the centrifuge pellets the DNA. The liquid poured off, leaving the pellet. It's washed with a 70% ethanol solution and air-dried.

Next, she adds the dried pellet to sterile water and incubates the sample at 98.6 F (average body temperature) to dissolve the pellet. Rose-Marie stores the solution at 39 F for a short time and -4F for longer term.

The next day, Dr. Turner prepares a reaction mix including the DNA sample of about 2-5 microns, a primer specific to human DNA, fluorescent dyes and PCR master mix. She loads the solution into a 96-well plate, seals it and places it in a real-time PCR instrument, programming a thermal cycling of 203F for 10 minutes, 40 cycles of 203F for 15 seconds and 140F for 1 minute. She measures the fluorescence during each cycle.

The next day brings analysis. She uses the lab's fluorometer to calculate the DNA concentration of the sample. Rose-Marie then compares the sample fluorescence to a standard curve, concentrating in nanograms and microliters.

The results for the sample are low (0.1-0.5 ng/μL), likely because of the silicone surface, environmental exposure, limited contact time, but likely enough to get a partial profile. She ran a further detailed analysis, but the result added little.

Rose-Marie studied the electropherogram on her monitor; the fluorescent peaks told their story in blues, greens, yellows, and reds. The mask fragment had yielded DNA—not much, and degraded from environmental exposure, but enough.

Thirteen loci. Not a full profile, but serviceable.

She'd run the sample through CODIS, and an hour later, the results populated her screen.

MATCH CONFIRMED Specimen ID: 2019-MO-KC-00847 Contributor: HARRIS, Gerald T. Match Probability: 1 in 4.7 million

That did it. They had their suspect identified with a 99.999979% of a positive match. The process had taken 6 days, even under priority status, but it garnered a result the agents in Kansas City would welcome!

Rose-Marie packaged and logged all information in LIMS, then took the package to the senior scientist of the labs, Toby Wilson, to communicate to the Kansas City office.

Chapter Eight

When Nicole Sheppard hung up the call with Dr. Wilson of the Quantico labs, she felt a rush of satisfaction. The evidence had left the office 8 days earlier. It might have been a month if she had not authorised the priority status. She called Agent McConnell and asked him to come to her office.

When Bruse arrived, he was attempting to keep his hope for positive results under control. He'd been an agent long enough to know the feeling of having hopes dashed by bad news. Yet, there was something in Sheppard's voice.

He knocked on her door and heard, "Come in, McConnell."

I le opened the door and took the seat she indicated.

"I just heard from Quantico. The DNA lab came through... we have a suspect. Gerald T. Harris. CODIS showed he had spent some time in an Illinois prison for robbery."

Bruce couldn't help a fist pump and a "Yes!"

Sheppard waited until his celebration ended. "Ahem... I want you to use Agents Philroy and Minzenmeyer to see if they can track down Harris. We find him, we'll find the others.

"Dr. Wilson from Quantico said the delivery of the official report should happen by the end of the week, but he's going to email me a summary. We use that to run down other leads. I want you to coordinate the efforts. Use whomever you need. This investigation is now priority one for this office. I'll forward you Dr. Wilson's email as soon as it hits.

"Let's also set up a meeting with the KCMPD as soon as we have something solid on the other elements of the case."

Sheppard pointed at the door to communicate that the meeting had ended. McConnell walked back out and went to find Philroy and Minzenmeyer.

Over the next several weeks, the investigators made several discoveries. Agents tracked down the printer ordered for Formlabs. They knew it shouldn't be a long list since the printer was medical grade and therefore expensive, ranging from $23,000 to $39,000. A printer matching the model and the timeframe before the first robbery sold to an address in Waynesburg, PA, about 50 miles from the first robbery in Wheeling, WV, paid for with a cashier's check.

Those agents got warrants for the records of the top three delivery companies in the Waynesburg area. FedEx delivered the printer. UPS had several records of orders from AliExpress to the same address. Agents deduced the shipments were of the resin for the molds and silicone rubber for the masks. It would take weeks and lots of bureaucracy red tape to serve a warrant on AliExpress, being a Chinese company, but in this case it seemed obvious. No PayPal or other e-payment system had records of payments for the items, so it seemed likely cryptocurrency had been used to finance the printer and supplies. Whoever ordered and received the shipments was not likely the financier of the operation.

Agents from the Pittsburgh office checked out the address. It was a rental property on the outskirts of the town. City records showed it was owned by a Patricia Rosen, an 82-year-old retired teacher. A local real estate company managed the property. The company rented the house to a man using the name Henry Ford, who paid six months' rent, cash up front. The man had lived there for only five months, enough time to accept the supply deliveries, and then he moved on. They got a copy of the renter's agreement signed by Henry Ford. A handwriting expert in Kansas City would check it at the appropriate time.

Pittsburgh's forensic team went with the agents to the address, now rented by a middle-aged named Brian and Janey King. Remarkably, the couple agreed to let the team check the house for prints once the agents explained the circumstances. They sat on the front porch drinking lemonade while the group moved freely inside the house. The forensic team found three prints that did not belong to either of the Kings. Agents both made notes to have the SAC in Kansas City write a letter of thanks to the Kings.

AFIS matched the prints to Harris. One more nail in the coffin.

McConnell requested a copy of Harris' intake documents from the warden at Southwestern Illinois Correctional Center in East St. Louis, IL, signed by the man himself. When it arrived, the bureau's lead handwriting expert compared the signatures of Gerald Harris and Henry Ford and determined the same person wrote them.

The agency went to the court, and the judge granted surveillance and digital forensic/email warrants for Harris.

Although they still had not located Harris, they were ready to follow him. The geeks in the digital forensics department tapped into Harris' Gmail account and found a treasure trove. He had stupidly kept all the email receipts for each purchase, including the printer and the mask supplies ordered from AliExpress.

Bruce went to Shepperd.

"It's time to bring in the KSMPD folks. They can help find Harris. It is him, no doubt."

They set up a meeting with Commander Powell, Chief Cobb and Sara for the next morning at the FBI offices.

McConnell opened the meeting with, "We have enough to arrest Gerald Harris once we locate him, but we feel surveillance is the best route to lead us to the rest."

Powell, Cobb and Sara looked at one another with smiles all round.

"What are we waiting for?" said Powell. "Let's get the bastards."

Chapter Nine

Tension in the KCMPD briefing room was approaching its palpable tensile limit. It wasn't about egos or showboating, but a readiness to bring everyone associated with the robbery investigation up to speed and talk about next steps.

Commander Lewis Powell was a cop with a tie instead of a gun. His work in the department meant he'd traded his bulletproof vest for the kind that went with a suit. He was already beyond his past-due date for retirement, but *once a cop, always a cop*, he'd say if the subject came up. Powell served in wars for the country and now served under the badge for the people of Kansas City. He was likable, with wispy white hair, sagging jowls, and kind eyes. Somehow, he'd outgrown the machismo of policing or ignored it.

Sara met the man only in passing and never conversed with him. But it was impossible to avoid his despising the fact of his department being hijacked by a federal bully in high heels.

The briefing room was at capacity. Powell stepped up to the lectern and cleared his throat. The room fell silent. The man had universal respect in the department.

"Nicole Sheppard is Special Agent in Charge," he said, introducing her passively. "Please give her the same consideration I expect from all my officers." With that, he found the chair again behind the lectern, near the rest of the department's leaders.

It was an assembly of ranking department heads and senior officers, with a smattering of feds. Usually, when administrative briefings happened, it was for special events, budgets, or bullshit. Sara wasn't part of that tier. She got hand-me-down news from either the watch commander or her direct supervisor. Both were present during this scheduled briefing. Being recalled from patrol by appointment meant Sara and Becca had no choice but to be there.

The Special Agent in Charge wasn't hard to look at, and a few of Sara's fellow officers had taken notice. Sheppard possessed considerable handsomeness and was somewhere between her late forties and mid-fifties, lean and mean. She wore black slacks and a black blazer over a crisp, deep crimson button-down shirt. She was no slouch, and the muted makeup complemented her age instead of disguising it.

"Thank you, Commander Powell," Sheppard said. The slits that were her eyes scanned the professionals waiting quietly for her to address them. She held a remote in her hand, her nails well manicured, and an expensive watch on her wrist. Behind her, the super-large flat screen mirrored the information she called up on the lectern's laptop. "As far as we know, this is the same particular group of cybercriminals who have been working their way from east to west across the country, starting in West Virginia and now in Kansas City."

As she spoke, she struggled as she tried to work the remote that activated the laptop, changing the photo on the presentation several times. It was like making three lefts to go right. The technology didn't seem overly complicated, but she needed to backtrack twice before landing on the desired photo. The fumble was exaggerated, considering Sheppard was such a hard-to-impress woman. Finally, the presentation showed the correct photo taken from the CCTV at the bank.

"The media dubbed the bank robbers the *Your Face Gang*, or YFG," she said with tonal abandon. It was lazy, durative, simple, and dangerous, meant to exploit fear and sell clickbait. But it was genuine and reliable. "Now, we've managed to cap the leaks to reporters about the criminals. So far, surprisingly, the media remains unaware of the latest evidence, except for the robberies and homicide at Boon Financial and Goodlife over the last couple of months."

"Well, ouch," Deputy Chief Ramona Cobb whispered. The word surprisingly was an unveiled dig at local department protocol.

As she spoke, various social media posts and news headlines appeared in rapid succession on the flat screen behind her. She continued to fumble the the remote for the laptop. A few muffled snickers echoed in the room.

When Sheppard's face tightened, the grip on the black remote tightened. Sara took her eyes off the woman, not wanting to witness technology defeating an agent. She reached down to stroke Becca's head.

The dog seemed more interested in the narcotics leader beside Special Agent Bruce McConnell. Or that's what Sara told herself. She glanced in McConnell's direction a few times, and each time, he'd been whispering to the man sitting next to him. Sara hoped Becca noticed the narcotics officer instead of McConnell because the man kept a shabby appearance. After all, criminals exhibiting criminal behavior expected the same from undercover cops. McConnell and the local narcotics team leader had hit it off immediately, and had been sharing snippet drug war stories instead of reviewing the recent case.

"Agent McConnell," Sheppard said, relenting to her Number Two.

His attention moved from the shabby officer, his gaze stopping at Sara for a second as he stood. He looked sharp in a two-piece suit, white shirt and black tie with just a whisper of pattern. The shirt clung tightly to his muscular chest but revealed nothing of his firm abdomen. He pulled at the jacket, buttoning the center button on the blazer before shouldering next to the SAC. She handed him the remote and whispered something. He kept smiling pleasantly. He nodded once and took over the presentation.

"I could have made three arrests by now on Highway 40," Lieutenant Charlie Bertrand said.

"I'll remember that for next month's budget meeting," Cobb said, unwilling to let that comment slide. Cobb sat to Bertrand's left, Sara to his right. Becca sat on the floor between the rows of chairs and the side table with condiments, drinks, and junk food from the local fast-food outlet. No one went near the table while Becca guarded it.

Bertrand was a stoic leader with bullet wounds and hardened features. Like most Hollywood leading men, he enjoyed a full head of hair and a constantly furrowed brow that balanced between frowning and quizzical. He plateaued at Lieutenant out of choice. For him to take a higher rank, he'd have to relocate. With a wife and two kids in high school, he chose to stay at Central instead of transferring to another city.

He kept bumping Sara's shoulder. At first, she thought it was accidental, but later, she realized it was his way of reminding her they were in a special meeting because of her work.

When Sheppard handed over the remote, McConnell abandoned it, relegating it to the other implements Sheppard brought with her. He touched a button on the laptop, and the flat projection showed the previous screen.

He used the laptop touchpad to show a picture of Keanu Reeves — youthful, beardless, dressed in a t-shirt and suit jacket; the face of the myriad 90s franchise films that launched the movie star icon.

"This is *not* our man," McConnell said, pointing at the screen. The photo changed to a shot from the bank's camera system, showing a picture that was a likeness of the action star. "Humans perceive visual technology straightforwardly and can see the creepy flaws that AI still hadn't perfected." Even Becca shook her head and chuffed. But it might have been to stay awake and not a commentary on the image.

"This," he said as he reached over and held up a mask for all to see, "is a relatively simple facsimile of the printed masks used by the thieves that made using widely available current 3D printing technology."

Someone'd posed for the image, their eyes now holes in the lifeless face, so similar and still so soulless. The only animated feature in the mask would be the eyes. Combined with a hoodie and sunglasses, the facsimile would pass as the real thing with ease.

"I want to remind you we're using local government-funded technology to create this mask," he said, smiling lightly as his eyes danced over the group. Sara reflexively smiled, fighting the urge. "So, that means the 'Your Face Gang' has access to far superior technology to make their masks."

The gathering mumbled. The image of a Formlab Form 4BL printer showed on the screen. It was sleek and large, designed for high-paying medical use.

"From the recovered sample, we discovered this," the image on the screen changed, "is the machine they used to make the masks." More images came up behind him in fluid contrast to Sheppard's meager presentation. "These masks have about an eighty percent error rate for facial recognition through CCTV tech, so don't expect to get much from the city's camera systems in finding these guys."

"How do you know they're all guys?" Jacqueline Richmond asked. The overnight watch commander drank coffee from a large travel thermos. "I mean, I know we're all *guys*, but come on, girls like to have fun too."

It raised the levity more notches than Sheppard made obvious she wanted from the group, but Richmond made a point.

"We know based on the interviews with victims," McConnell said. "We've been compiling enough information on the case to say with certainty all suspects are male."

He continued with another image. The mask went into the bag.

"This is the key to solving all our problems," McConnell said as his eyes rested on Sara. The following image was of Becca, wearing her service medal, posing for the portrait. "Our lead investigator cracked the entire case for us."

The crowd of LEOs all applauded.

The next image generated a flash of embarrassed heat from Sara because it was something she didn't know existed. An adventurous photographer at the USPCA Region One competition caught a surreptitious picture of Sara in a kneeling shooter stance in combat boots, shorts, polo, and ball cap in profile with Becca. She and Becca watched something unseen in the image, their focus intense.

Sara rested her hand on Becca's shoulder as the dog sat up attentively as a sudden and enthusiastic round of applause erupted in the briefing room.

"Sergeant O'Shea and K9 Officer Becca returned to Goodlife Financial the night of the robbery-homicide. I was there, but I didn't help," McConnell said. "Officer Becca worked some canine magic through that amazing nose, finding the tiny scrap of mask left behind by one suspect." As he spoke, FBI evidence photos of the small piece of mask appeared on the screen behind him, along with a map that retraced the path Becca took that led to the crucial evidence in the case. "In a very rushed job, the FBI crime lab's testing of this scrap of material evidence led us to a breakthrough, and after nine days, you are all here."

"Once processed, the DNA led us to the mask wearer's identity, and we began linking him to other criminals known to be associates." The screen went dramatically dark before five different images of unknown individual males appeared across the screen. Each came up in a programmed array, each image culled from social media except for one.

The other images melted off the screen, and a mugshot with a criminal record appeared on the right.

"This man, we think, is the leader of the gang," McConnell said. The man looked unwashed and rugged, with neck tattoos and a gaunt face, like he'd struggled with substance abuse. "Gerry Harris, thirty-eight, the one identified through DNA at Quantico. He spent four years in a minimum-security prison and got out on early parole when he secured a remote job working in a data center. He was good with phones and computers."

The next image showed a man in his mid-forties, tipping toward fifty, thin-lipped and laid-back. The picture caught him shopping at a department store, possibly the same store near Goodlife Financial.

"This is William Wilson, but his social media profiles have him listed as Butch, also employed at the same remote call center. They're required to have conference calls weekly. We haven't secured a warrant to listen in on those call recordings to link them, but from what we've been able to piece together, we don't have to because..." McConnell spoke as he switched to a new picture that involved the prior intro-duced suspects and four more.

It was a scene in a classy restaurant. Other than the errant facial hair, the men were looking sharp in suits. They were celebrating something with four other men. One black man, Wilson, sat in profile in the surveillance photo.

"...this is a critical picture because, ladies and gentlemen, we believe you're looking at the Your Face Gang, unmasked," he said.

"Yeah, they're sitting in the Stone Bridge," Cobb said. "I've been there. It takes a month to get a reservation."

"Our team went in as busboys and servers, collecting everything from their table. We collected fingerprints and/or DNA. Our team tipped the maître d' a C-note out of our field office Christmas party fund, so this year, we can only afford grape juice." The quip got more laughs as Sheppard shifted in her chair. "We think, Chief Cobb, the point of that dinner was to celebrate the latest bank robbery."

"That's brazen," someone said behind Sara. She didn't bother pin-pointing, watching McConnell and the images of the men who used violence to beat the stable system of economics and commerce.

"It is, but who are they? No one in that place knows they're bank robbers. They don't seem at all concerned the last job got people killed."

The next set of images showed up with social media account images of the dinner guests.

"Now, we think the rest of the men in the gang are: Michael Estel, 33, out of Chicago. He has a juvenile record but hasn't been in the system since." The black man's prominent image changed to a pair of young men playing junior basketball in a call center with a tiny hoop mounted to a cubicle wall. "These two men are Peter and Oliver Newkirk—"

"Are they brothers?" the wisecracker asked from the back. Mc-Connell bore responsibility for the levity and lightened the group enough to make commentary.

"No," McConnell said, not missing a beat before pointing to someone over Sara's left shoulder. Becca glanced, thinking the motion was something she should follow. "Yes," he added. "Good one."

"Alright, can it," Sheppard said. "Get on with it." Her mouth tightened around two words she held back from the audience: *Number Two.*

"They are the computer geeks behind the programming used to hack the system, and the ones using the 3D printing equipment. They don't have even a parking ticket between them, but we think they are up to their necks in the robberies and are probably the ones who chose the equipment and had it sent to Harris in Pennsylvania. These two have the brains to create the scenarios for the robberies.

"However, we are still fuzzy on the hierarchy in the gang. We think the financing comes from outside the group. Our digital forensic folks could not backtrack to discover the funding source, mainly because of the use of cryptocurrency."

The image again changed, now to the FBI logo.

Sheppard took over, standing and straightening her ironed black blazer. McConnell sat down again and sipped coffee.

"So, through the intricate detective work of the FBI, we've been able to use additional DNA taken from the mask piece found by Sergeant O'Shea's partner and fast-tracked it to identify Gerald Harris."

Sara lifted her hand.

Sheppard hesitated and almost rolled her eyes before addressing her. The look suggested Sheppard expected Sara to give credit to

Becca. But Sheppard didn't acknowledge the K9 as an officer. "Yes, Sergeant?"

"Can we go back to the restaurant photo?"

McConnell stepped up without request and sent the laptop back to the photo Sara asked for.

"You left one out," she said, pointing at the screen and adding, "at the dinner table."

On the screen, a man with his back to the camera talked to Michael Estel privately.

"Who is that man?"

"We don't know. If he left any fingerprints or DNA, we haven't identified him yet," Sheppard said. "Our programs haven't linked him to any of the other member's social media accounts. We believe he could be the group's bank, but that is just speculation. We're still processing data, and you'll get it in real-time when we get it."

"Okay, we found and started a tail on Harris, which led us to a neighborhood in Gladstone, Missouri, but the tail lost him. Sergeant O'Shea and Officer Becca," Sara thought she could see Sheppard's mouth tighten when McConnell used Becca's title, "posing as a dog and owner out for a stroll, picked up Newkirk's trail from a paper cup he'd dropped before the tail lost him."

Sara's concentration waned as she remembered their walk. Becca, nose down, following the scent of the cup's user, looked a bit too, not a pet being walked. Almost as if reading her thoughts, Becca moved into the grass to a tree, lifted her back leg and relieved herself, marking her territory. "Good girl," Sara had quipped. Becca finished and then turned and walked back the way they had come.

The dog's behavior confused Sara. Becca was acting as if she had finished tracking in the middle of the job. When Sara didn't follow, Becca sat looking into Sara's eyes. That's when the light bulb went on. Becca had finished tracking the prep, saying so by her marking the house.

"Officer Becca led us to this house." The image again changed to a common ranch-style house.

Sheppard exchanged looks with Chief Cobb. The woman took her cue and stood as Sara and McConnell exchanged glances. She wondered if he thought the same as she did: the unknown suspect was the mastermind. Even if Gerry Harris served as manager, the last man with his short, curly brown hair and military neck buzz was likely the one who really called all the shots.

"Let's all appreciate the swift efforts of the FBI's Forensic Lab, the local and Pittsburgh FBI field office agents and the direct attention of Special Agent in Charge Sheppard," Chief Cobb said as the audience gave half-hearted applause. "When you leave this room, you will have access to all this data, plus Commander Lewis Powell will take over to brief you at deployment. He's working closely with the FBI HRT commander to coordinate a joint venture between agencies to make the arrests." Cobb paused, looking a little worried.

The FBI dropped the Special Weapons and Tactics (SWAT) nomenclature for something more heroic for public consumption, so it adopted the Hostage Rescue Team (HRT). That worked well because the KCMPD assault team's nickname 'T-Rats' ignited explosive media coverage.

"I don't need to remind anyone this group has crossed several homicidal lines they cannot return from," Cobb said. "I have authorized Sergeant O'Shea and Becca's involvement in the raid. The bad guys have killed. We know they can use guns, but so can every idiot out there. Don't expect them to show restraint, but don't be cowboys out there either." Cobb glanced around. Her soft amber eyes found Sara. "The details of this briefing must remain confined to the members of this room. Thank you for your efforts, especially Sergeant O'Shea and Officer Becca."

Chapter Ten

KCMPD's Tactical Response Team, or as they preferred to be called, *T-Rats*, was one of the best in the country, smooth like gun oil on firearms. With the FBI HRT team involved, there were a few pieces of grit in the lubricant.

It felt different that night.

The team leaders from both agencies had agreed on other plans for insertion. A storm roiled across the high plains. The tension was like static electricity stroking the grain fields ahead of snowstorms. Snow capped off the city like a whipped topping, making road travel difficult. The governor issued a severe winter weather warning, asking travelers to stay home. After taking into consideration the unexpected change of weather, the team leaders finally agreed on a final plan.

Both tactical teams sat in the large mobile forward command vehicle. It was the size of a large trailer on wheels, a glorified RV. But from inside the command center was an amazingly efficient way to direct any kind of operation.

Some tactical commanders considered the Witching Hour the best time to breach. But Commander Lewis Powell referred to the Bitching Hour as a better time. Midnight was cliché, and most people who robbed banks for a living likely didn't worry about setting morning alarm clocks. So, 4 AM was a better time because even bad guys needed to sleep sometime.

"Alright, last time," Commander Lewis Powell said.

He took a breath, giving the KCMPD T-Rats and FBI HRT a chance to cease talking individually. Everyone's head was in the game; most were checking each other's tactical gear. Powell stood beside a large flat screen and the tabletop version of the same data. He focused on the flat screen.

"The eggheads gave us the data we needed to link four individuals," he said. "Later, we'll buy the science geeks beers. Right now, let's get in, grab, and get out." Three individuals appeared on the screen. "Gerry Harris, William Wilson, aka Butch, and Michael Estel are all reportedly at the residence. It's likely the Newkirk twins are there as well, but there may be others."

Various social media posts cropped to show only faces appeared following surveillance photos of the men gathering in different eateries around the city.

"Hey, I go there. They have good duck soup," Bernie Duarte said. He was barely audible, meant for the team members at the back, but Powell's bullet-gray eyes found him like a sniper checking a target. Duarte was young, with a muscle-bound physique that somehow matched his mentality. He wasn't the type of guy Sara would ever want to know personally.

She'd served with plenty of men and women she didn't get along with on the job. But Duarte was young—youngest on the T-Rats. He was eager to show force, to prove his abilities trumped his inexperience, which made him feel inferior to the others, and Sara thought that made him dangerous, but would never voice that opinion.

"Neither of the Newkirk's have a criminal history. The FBI techs think these two are the cyber masterminds, but no one's seen either of them since the aborted tail, and their social media accounts have gone completely silent."

With Becca's diligence, the FBI cracked the case, and KCMPD would make headlines as the joint task force to take them down. YFG hitting banking computers inside branches and hacking the system was unique. Bypassing security protocols with old-fashioned violence in the age of data theft with bank teller masks meant they cased the targets well ahead of hitting the places.

No branch manager making little better than minimum wage ever said *no* to a gun in the face when someone demanded to gain entry to the computer systems. Did Lowell Petersen ever think he'd see a gun in his face? Did he think he'd get caught embezzling? Some employees complained of long-term stress attributed to the bank robbers. No one expected to get held up at work, but they trained for it. Some employees immediately quit following the hack and grab.

The YFG *modus operandi* was stunning. What a nightmare it must have been for employees to ask to help the next person in line and look into your own face and the business end of a semiautomatic gun. A place like Chicago uses over 25,000 surveillance cameras. Kansas City owned significantly less. The YFGs would eventually move out of the area. Hopefully after tonight, they wouldn't get the chance.

Becca's nose led to a break in DNA identification, along with tenacious CSI and FBI prioritizing, law enforcement identified their suspects and a current hideout. All that resolve led the HRT and KCMPD's T-Rats right to the bad guys' front door.

"They are dangerous. They have killed without conscience," Powell said, glancing around at eager faces. "Treat them with the same deference as you would any hostile target. One other thing. We'd like to take the twins alive. Without them, the entire scheme falls apart. But do not risk LEO lives. If they pose an imminent threat to your lives, take them out."

The images wiped from the screen, replaced by the exterior view of the three-bedroom house in Gladstone, Missouri—four blocks away and a scenic thirty-minute drive from the Heart of America.

"Their house has three bedrooms, two bathrooms, and a two-car garage," Powell said. The team was restless, ready to roll. "From what the FBI gathered, it's rented to an alias, probably set up by the brothers. It's got a finished basement, with the nearest house six blocks from the target residence." Powell brought up interior schematics. "We will go in two six-man teams."

"Team One is FBI HRTs, and Team Two is T-Rats. HRT will breach the front, and T-Rats hit the back simultaneously. Please do *not* shoot your teammates; I don't want the paperwork. Converge here." He jabbed a finger at the living room floor plan. "After you've cleared all other rooms, upstairs and down. Check your corners; don't expect anyone to be asleep. We've counted six exterior cameras marked here."

The screen changed to the overhead exterior view, showing the red highlighted dots for cameras and the speculative area of coverage for each. The overhead image was current, another gift from the FBI. They used whisper drones for flyovers, scanning the area with IR and pictures to update the property view.

"These spots," he pointed to the dead zones across the yards, "show what we hope are blind spots in their system. We didn't expect snow, so we'll stand out like black silhouettes in all that white. We expect a lot of drifting, so take your time." Powell grunted, expelling frustration.

"Let's assume they have more cameras we're not seeing. When we get boots on the ground, you have thirty seconds to converge, breach, and make arrests. Let's make that forty seconds based on snow depth."

He was wrapping up and ready to call time, but Sara O'Shea pushed forward, jabbing a finger at the exterior picture of the house showing in the lower section of the flat screen.

"What, O'Shea?" Powell asked, impatiently.

"That's the basement access from the outside," Sara said, shifting her tactical gear. She was already sweaty, but it didn't matter. She used the mouse pad to isolate and enhance the house's side and the flat rectangle under the window. "That's the side basement entrance. See how it's inclined slightly up the outer wall. You can see its outline in the bushes."

"A third entrance?" Powell asked, looking at Lieutenant Charlie Bertrand and the FBI HRT commander. "How did we miss it?"

"It's covered with weeds," the FBI agent said dismissively.

"They probably never use it," Duarte said. "There's one like it at my mom's house. It's sealed up."

"Well," growled Powell, "we should consult your mommy, eh, Duarte?" Knowing the comment was embarrassing was impossible to miss, but it helped break the tension.

Powel growled with exasperation. "We simply don't have the manpower to cover three entrances." He turned to his FBI counterpart and said, "We fucked this, didn't we?"

"Give me another person and Becca and I can handle the basement incursion," Sara said coldly.

"Bullshit," said the HRT commander. "We're not sending in a team that under-manned."

Powell thought for a minute he didn't have and said almost under his breath, "We cannot afford to have any egress uncovered. We could lose half the YFG if they just happen to be in the basement."

He looked at Sara, then Becca, and shook his head as he said reluctantly, "Alright, Sergeant O'Shea. Since you found it, you and Officer Becca are *now* Team Three. And you, Duarte, go along and, for God's sake, follow Sergeant O'Shea's orders. You are to breach the exterior basement door. If it does not open, proves locked, or appears disused, you will move to the back and cover Team Two. Do not take unnecessary risks. Clear?"

"Yes, sir," O'Shea said and glanced at Duarte.

Duarte wasn't watching her. For a change, his eyes went to her feet, to O'Shea's tactical partner. The Belgian Malinois lay prone and alert, waiting more patiently than anyone else. Her bright brown eyes scanned the group, but she relied on her nose more than what she saw. She knew the team, and the team, even Duarte, respected Becca as an enforcer in the group.

"I am leading Team One," the FBI agent said, lifting his hand to signal his group. "Lieutenant Bertrand is leading Team Two. Let's move out."

The command center's back doors opened, and the officers and agents poured out and tore through the pristine snow, rushing away toward the target home.

Chapter Eleven

Becca, with her short fawn-colored hair, black face, and black rubberized boots, slipped silently through the deep snow toward the basement door. Sara pushed her legs through the knee-high drifts to forge a path, never bringing her boot higher than the snow. Becca kept pace, leading Sara, moving stealthily and on high alert. The dog stopped and chuffed; Sara paused, with Duarte too close behind. He bumped into her once, twenty yards from the house, and Sara turned and quietly set him straight.

She hastily whispered, "Listen, this is the one time I'll allow you to look at my ass," she hissed. "You keep your distance; you move only after we move. Don't step outside the path we've cut. You stop when we stop. If you're watching my ass, you're following Becca. She will get us where we need to go, got it?"

Duarte's flashy grin might even be too bright for nighttime tactical gear, lighting up in the one-eye IR piece from her helmet. He nodded. He was supposed to wear a black face mask, but Sara wasn't reminding the young man of something he should already know.

Orders went out in her ear. The teams moved like a single organism, surrounding the access points with quiet precision. Sara, Becca, and Duarte saw Team Two slip around the back corner of the house, moving single file to the back door.

Sara knew they would pause momentarily, with the leaders side-stepping to let the *Donker* do its job. The specially designed battering ram snapped deadbolts like pencils. Sara didn't need one to breach the sloping black door. She and Becca continued onward, losing sight of Team Two to get into position at the metal basement egress. She crouched, heart hammering so hard it beat against the earpiece as she listened.

"Breach! Breach," came the command from Powell.

There came a simultaneous crash from the front and back of the house as the dual Donkers broke through the doors. Inside, she heard the teams converge, shouting in her earpiece and through the walls. When gunfire started inside, Sara wanted to sprint to the back door, and it caused her to hesitate. Becca tensed between her legs, expecting Sara to make the first move. Becca used Sara's body language to read the scenario. Duarte stumbled two steps before the first shots hit. Sara ducked instinctively. But Becca lay prone, head up, staring at the basement door.

Through the night vision eyepiece, Sara could see a handle. The rusted steel double doors angled up from the weed-choked ground to approximately two feet into the foundation wall. Snow covered most of the rusty paint. Anyone sneaking around the property would likely not see the door, especially in the dark. She began digging for the edges. Becca slipped a step away into the snow, staring at the basement door. She knew better than Sara.

"We need to get inside," Duarte whispered, leaning closer to Sara, eager to make a historic arrest.

"Becca says no."

"That damned dog doesn't talk," Duarte said, raising his voice an octave above a whisper.

"She talks to me," Sara said, leaning forward, slipping her tactical glove under the outside flap of the steel door.

It was nearly impossible to lift the door one-handed. It moved freely, four inches. Sara's right arm quivered at the hyper-extended attempt to lever the door open enough for Becca, herself, and possibly her inexperienced third.

Becca shifted against Sara's leg, using their sign language to alert her. Hot air erupted from the opening, turning to steam when the hot air clashed violently with the cold snowstorm gusts.

Sara closed the steel door against her glove before pulling her hand out. More gunfire erupted inside, muffled through insulation and closed windows. Some T-Rats used the Remington semi-automatic .233 rifle. The bark from the Remington possessed a distinct twang. And inside, some rifles returned fire after the powerful shotgun blasts started the argument.

Duarte carried a sidearm Glock and cradled the M4a1, ready to lift and shoot as needed. When Sara glanced at her human partner, Duarte pointed the M4 carbine at the closed and covered windows in the house—too many to cover simultaneously.

"Get over here," Sara whispered, pointing at the double doors hiding in the deep drifts. The wind slapped her face, forcing her eyes closed momentarily. "Get this open."

"Shit, O'Shea. We need to get to the back door and backup the team," Duarte spat.

"Get over here and open this *now*!"

Duarte wanted to break point and break protocol. She ranked above him. He was a rookie, as far as she was concerned. Sara thought anyone besides Becca was a rookie because she trained with her four-legged predator. Everyone else was second, even if Sara wouldn't admit it to her team or the department's shrink.

Duarte slung the carbine and crouched beside Sara. He glanced at Becca, who focused on the trapdoor. He hadn't been that close to a Belgian Malinois before. Becca already ignored the man, even though Duarte saw her as sleek terror incarnate. She was formidable in her K9 black ballistic vest, even if she didn't flash those dazzling canines.

"Ready," Sara said.

She lifted her weapon of choice: the Sig Sauer 9mm. The P226 MK25 served with Sara in the military and department cleared to carry. The Sig carried Siglite night sights and a 15-round steel mag. She could shoot a gnat's eye at twenty feet.

Duarte curled his gloves under the cold steel lip and heaved. The door opened like a rectangular metal mouth, showing a black mouth and concrete teeth leading into the dark. Hinges groaned.

"Shit," Sara hissed. "Don't let that door slam against the bushes."

She stood to help Duarte lean the gate against the dormant bush, branches clawing at the rusty steel-like nails on a chalkboard.

The velvet gap down the throat showed no lights or movement. She tossed on illumination flare down into the darkness, but it failed to trigger. Hot air rushed at her, smelling of closed-in space and humans. It took five strides to clear ten steps. Becca cleared the space in a second, Sara did it in two, and Duarte took three seconds to step. The tread on his boots compacted snow, causing him to slip and eventually stumble downstairs. It was loud, clattering, and clacking. Overhead, boots ran hither and thither, shouting and shooting, chaos, bedlam.

Becca sidestepped, glancing behind her as Duarte's helmet banged against the concrete floor. Sara kneeled, turning, ready to assist Duarte on his feet. She heard Becca's alert snapping bark. The warning came in the same second as automatic gunfire exploded all around them.

Sara tried recovering, half diving and half running to cover Becca. Becca made a sound that caused Sara to cry out. The dog's yelp was louder than even the constant barrage of angry firelights sparking from a single point. Bullets peppered the cinderblock walls, floor, and stairs. Bullets slammed into Sara like speeding hornets, slapping the breath out of her lungs before she could take one. She felt a searing heat stabbing her left arm. More impacts against her chest drove her back and sideways, still diving for her partner.

Duarte's cries from the darkness and concrete dust started strong before they sharply went silent. One second he was alive, screaming, then the sudden stop to his pained voice made Sara's balled stomach lurch.

She rolled with the impact of the bullets. They slammed into her midsection. Scattering across the Kevlar back and chest plate. When the bullets stopped, it was nearly as abrupt as Duarte's last cry. The spent magazine clattered to the floor in the dark, roughly fifteen to twenty feet away.

She heard nothing in the ringing silence. The concrete dust made the yawning darkness suddenly opaque. Snow flurries spilled into the opening as a gusting, frigid wind swirled with plaster dust, cordite, and the smell of blood. She saw nothing in the dark. Lying on the floor, she didn't move and could barely breathe. Every breath was like another knifepoint stabbing her ribs. Her right hand still held the 9mm with military training, screwing muscles and bones to the weapon. Sara's arm dragged from under her, pointing into the void.

Sara rolled and crawled to where Becca lay unmoving. Training overrode panic. Hard-wiring of tactical muscle memory hammered down most emotional impulses. Sara shifted, leaning back until she felt Becca's still form against her back as she leveled the gun. Sara let the Sig Sauer 9mm find its target.

In the dark, she heard hurried whimpers. The clatter and snap of a fresh magazine into the civilian version of AR-15, customized into a lethal idiot gun, followed by the *cha-chink* of death, allowed Sara to zero in on the target, even in the dark.

She fired two shots. Both made soft, solid impacts. She didn't need to see the target. The AR-15 clattered to the floor. The target's groaning, anxious, ragged breathing drew closer. Sara tensed, watching through the roiling dust and blowing snow illuminated in the dimness of the snow's reflected light from the open portal, for the figure to emerge like a horrible monster from some bad movie.

Sara watched the ground view of the bare feet, ugly toes slapping the cold concrete as the figure lurched forward. Behind her, Becca made a noise, alerting Sara to the combatant. Her blood ran cold since Becca didn't rise, run, jump, or bite. Her partner was seriously injured, her breach team member was likely dead, and the combatant staggered into limited view.

His left hand pressed against the white T-shirt with K-Pop members embroiled amid a tie-dye Jackson Pollock rendition of blood spatter. The right hand carried a lighter, more manageable secondary weapon than the AR-15.

Sara stared at the threat, seeing the man thought he'd get to the door and make it to the exit, but didn't expect to see Duarte's body. He didn't see Sara until he tracked her boots to the left using the snow's ambiance and saw the deadly end of the SIG Sauer P226 ready to shout.

Sara'd never been great at communicating with people. Becca and she shared an intrinsic language that went beyond talking. But Becca couldn't protect Sara now. It was Sara's turn to save her partner. Training kicked in before Sara knew she'd spoken.

"Drop it." Two words were enough to convey the message with more meaning than firing a two-cent round.

Instead of complying, Oliver Newkirk raised the pistol as he sniffled, blinking back the streaming tears. Sara had put two close group rounds into his belly, so close he could cover them with one hand.

She didn't hesitate, didn't wait for him to finish leveling the gun. Instead, Sara put the third bullet into the blank forehead, leaving a perfect circle of 9mm. Oliver's head snapped back before his brain registered what happened. The body smacked against the ground as the back of his skull splattered over the concrete.

The gunfire ceased upstairs. Sara ignored the stinging fire searing through the armor of her gear. She flopped onto her back and to her left side, holstering the pistol before throwing off her gloves. Her fingers went through the fur. She felt wetness. Becca breathed, panting—no whining, no sound, just panting.

Sara lifted her head to ensure her throat mic and the open basement projected her following two words: "Officer down!"

Chapter Twelve

Nothing mattered except Becca. Sara's vocal cords went hoarse, screaming for EMTs and strategic help. The basement, suddenly illuminated as several individuals rushed to the basement from outside and the stairs. The lights showed a segmented set of rooms and a washer and dryer close to the basement egress to the outside. Sara pressed her hands against the bullet hole in Becca's belly. The amateur gunman shot randomly and wildly, yet he'd hit Bernie Duarte and critically injured K9 Officer Becca.

Someone attempted to separate Sara from Becca to get to Sara's wounds, but she refused to move away. The EMTs focused on Duarte. They ignored Becca. Sara cried, shouted, swore, and demanded they save Becca, but protocol for K9s wasn't a top priority. If Duarte's heart still beat, he would be the first to go on the gurney.

"Sara, you're injured," Lieutenant Charlie Bertrand's voice and large hands gripped Sara by the shoulders. More lights erupted around her. Flashlights and high-powered stage lights ignited the space. "You need medical attention."

"No, Becca first," she said. "You get them to help Becca."

Bertrand stood upright. He was over six feet tall in his full tactical gear and weighed two hundred and twenty pounds of commanding muscle. He keyed the throat mic and spoke, watching Becca and Sara.

Sara wedged herself against Becca, cradling the dog, so the pressure applied was constant and kept her immobile. A second group of EMTs carried a backboard down the exterior stairwell.

"Over here," Bertrand said, directing the man and woman to Sara. "Get her up, get her to the hospital. I've got emergency crews heading to the hospital now."

"You need to let go of the dog, ma'am," the heavyset woman said, crouching by Sara. "I need to see where you're injured."

"Not me, you idiot," Sara said, swinging her arm free of the EMT. The movement was like curling a knife in the muscle. "Becca. You need to take Becca."

"We're not allowed to transport do—" The technician stopped talking when Bertrand grabbed his elbow.

"Shut up, get Becca stabilized on that backboard, and get her in your ambulance now. That's not a dog. That's a police officer."

"I need to clear it with—"

"No. You do it. Now!" The EMT recognized Bertrand's bark was less substantial than his bite.

Sara reluctantly moved away from Becca. The dog's head lulled out of her arms. She gasped and shivered, seeing her partner's eyes slowly close. The EMTs used advanced clotting gauze on the bullet hole under the hem of the dog's bulletproof vest. The lead tech left the vest on, using a second hemostatic gauze bandage to secure the site. He checked Becca's other side to see if the bullet had gone through and through. He shook his head at the woman. The bullet went in and didn't come out.

"I'll help you move her onto the board," Sara said. But when she attempted to move her left arm, it refused to obey. It was limp, sliding against the floor as she sat up.

"Sara, I'll do it," Bertrand said, crouching with the lead tech to lift Becca in a two-person move while the woman slid the board under Becca.

Blood seeped across the floor and pooled under Becca. The golden fur was red with matted blood from coagulating.

"How is Bernie?" Sara struggled to ask. She couldn't see the rookie with the swarm of people around him.

"Let's get you up," Bertrand said. Gently, like a surrogate father, he lifted Sara. She was cold; chills ran through her, and goosebumps peppered her skin. Her teeth chattered. "We need to get you to the hospital. You're shot."

"What? No, I'm going with Becca."

"Yes, you are. Let's get upstairs."

Cold, gusting wind assaulted her sweaty face, freezing the tears on her cheeks. Snowflakes clung to her eyelashes. She lost her footing, and her head swooned. Around her, people were talking and shouting. She couldn't see them and barely understood them. Someone lifted her off her feet.

In and out of consciousness, Sara woke to swaying movement, the scream of ambulance sirens.

The rocking of the vehicle under the locked wheels of the gurney jostled her, bringing her back to consciousness. She blinked several times and swiped away the plastic oxygen mask, turning her head in a panic. Beside her, Becca lay strapped to a backboard on the second gurney. Her tongue lolled out of her muzzle.

The female EMT focused on Sara's bullet wound. They'd cut off her vest, shed her utility belt, and taken her weapons. Becca was without her vest, but wore her collar, looking like a deflated version of the strong-spirited animal that made her the best partner Sara could ever have.

She reached out with her right hand and touched Becca's foreclaw. Sara fought to keep her eyes open and lost the battle.

When she woke again, the EMT and Bertrand were shouting at each other outside the open doors. Sara saw Becca was missing. In a fright, she tried sitting up. Belted down on the gurney, she could barely move.

"Becca!" Sara's shout and movement inside the ambulance caused it to sway.

Bertrand appeared over her, looking down, touching her forearm. "We're at Mission Emergency," he said. "They took Becca inside. I want to get you to the hospital."

"No, damn it. Let me up," she said. "I need to get inside."

"You're no good to her if you bleed out," Bertrand said. "They can take you to..."

"Charlie, please, I need to be with Becca. She saved my life."

Bertrand blinked at her. His jaw muscles tensed as he shifted to look at the waiting crew.

"Let her up." Bertrand climbed out of the ambulance. "Don't argue with her. If you can't stay to tend to her, get another ambulance out here."

The female tech said nothing to Sara, glaring at her as she undid the straps. Bertrand helped Sara stumble out of the ambulance after she rolled off the gurney. He supported her as they went inside.

Mission Veterinary Emergency and Specialty (MVES) provided emergency animal services for Kansas City. Open every day of the year, at all hours; filled with compassionate and experienced veterinarians who handled more than wounded K9 duty.

Once in the lobby, Bertrand directed Sara to sit, but one technician at the counter saw the hemostatic gauze bandages on Sara's arm. She directed Bertrand to a private room with Sara. Once inside, Sara fought to stay aware. The adrenaline turned to acid in her veins. The pounding headache and lack of control in the uncertain environment caused her to faint again. Maybe it was the blood loss.

She regained consciousness prone on the floor. Something cushioned her head from the concrete floor. It smelled of dog urine and antiseptic.

"She needs to get to the hospital," a woman said heatedly over her.

"As soon as we know about Becca," Bertrand said. "You get Becca stable, and I'll get Sara out of here."

Someone examined her arm. "She needs to get to surgery. If that bullet nicked an artery, or if it nicked a nerve, she might lose the use of her arm. I'm not a surgeon of people."

"Where's Becca?" Sara didn't need to open her eyes to speak to the bickering people hovering over her. She couldn't get the room to stop spinning when she opened her eyes.

"Becca's in surgery," the veterinarian said. "That's where you should be. You're not doing her any good by being here. It looks like the bullet perforated Becca's liver. We have one of the best surgeons in four states here today because, lucky for Becca, the Midwest Veterinarian Collaboration Conference is this week."

A cold stethoscope bell pressed against Sara's chest. Fingers pinched her wrist. After a few seconds, the fingers released and pried open her eyelid. She saw a stabbing LED penlight.

"Sergeant O'Shea, your commander tells me you're an exemplary officer. He says you follow directions better than most people under him. He tells me that Becca is as much a part of the police department as any other officer. But I can't assist Becca in surgery if I'm out here dealing with a stubborn police officer covered in blood, scaring the other patrons in my lobby. Do yourself a favor, do Becca a favor, and let the lieutenant take you to the hospital so I can do my job to save your partner's life."

Her recovery from surgery made it difficult to focus. There was a lot of fuzz in Sara's brain. She'd lost track of time and her whereabouts. One minute, she was in the emergency veterinary clinic; the next, strapped to another gurney in an ambulance.

The vehicle rocked and swung around corners. At one point, the brakes came on hard, with a blaring horn, and Sara stirred to consciousness because the pressure in her head made it feel like it would pop off her shoulders.

When she woke again, somewhere sterile and quiet, terror caught in her throat because she couldn't see Becca. Where was she?

"Hey, anyone there?" she called. Ugly patterned curtains surrounded her. The nasal cannula around her ears, poking her nostrils, felt like a plastic snake that coiled around her face. She pulled at it. "Hey, where am I?"

The curtain shifted. The door beyond opened and closed, creating a slight wind tunnel in the room, playing on the drapes. A woman of obvious Indian heritage smiled at her. Wearing scrubs and a hairnet, with the lanyard around her neck holding all the information. Sara didn't want to focus.

"It's alright, you're safe. There is a cop outside the door," she said. "Do you know who you are?"

"Do you know who *you* are?" Two can play that game. "Where am I?"

"I'm Dr. Rajgopal," she said. "I was your surgeon. You're in the University of Kansas Hospital. And now it's your turn."

It was a stupid game, and she didn't want to play it. Sara draped her right arm over her eyes, recumbent on the hospital bed. "I'm Sara O'Shea, and I want to see Becca."

"Very good," Rajgopal said. She made notes on a laptop that might have been there all along, but Sara'd missed it. "You're in recovery. That arm will be immobile for the next twenty-four to forty-eight hours. You will need extensive physical therapy."

"Yeah, yeah, yeah, where's Becca?"

"Your Lieutenant Bertrand and a few others have been waiting for your response from surgery. Do you have any family we should contact?"

"I don't know." Sara blinked at the doctor. "Can you answer me about Becca or not?"

The smile on the woman's face might have been for cruel effect, and if not tied down to the bed, she might have wrist-locked the woman to get her answers. "I was not your K9 partner's surgeon," she said. "I heard about the hijacking of the ambulance to transport her to the pet hospital."

"Nero's Law," Sara blurted. The heart monitor on her left hiccupped with her heart rate as annoying questions abounded. "Massachusetts law requires K9 officers access to an ambulance or helicopter in case of shootings."

"I was unfamiliar with that particular law, and the last time I looked, we're in Kansas, not Massachusetts."

"I just want to see Becca."

"What about humans? Do you want to see any of them?" she asked. "I have so many cops in my lobby that anyone seeking emergency services today better not have an outstanding warrant."

"I don't care. You can let anyone in that will get me out of here so I can see Becca."

Dr. Rajgopal nodded, made more notes on the laptop, closed it, parked it under her arm, then said, "Stay calm, Sara, and we'll get you healed," and disappeared through the curtain again. Sara breathed heavily, feeling the stinging beats where the bullets slammed into the protective vest. Alone behind the curtain, she pulled back the sheet and lifted the surgical gown so she could see the damage. There were several bruises peppering her chest and surely reflected on her back as well. Under her left breast, there was a distinct line progressing across her ribs in an upward trajectory that ended in a heavily bandaged arm.

The door opened, the curtain again swayed, and Sara covered up. The next face she saw was a disembodied head of an FBI agent smiling at her. He opened the curtains to step through. Special Agent Bruce McConnell walked to her right bedside. He gripped the steel bed bar. Under his left arm was a computer tablet. Following him was Lieutenant Bertrand.

"You're popular today," he said. "Sheppard's going ahead with the press conference with Deputy Chief Cobb without you or me."

"What's going on with Becca?" she asked, sucking back tears, breaking down to a whisper. "Please, Charlie," speaking to Bertrand, "tell me, is she okay?"

"She is coming along well. I'm more concerned about you at the moment. You know you're a pain in the ass, right?"

Sara nodded, then said through tear-filled eyes, "I don't remember a lot, Lieutenant, but I remember Becca got care because of you, and I will never forget that."

"Becca's one of my best officers. I'm not gonna let anything happen to her. Now you get some rest so we can get you up and around to cause more trouble." He reached across and squeezed her hand

and smiled. "I've got to go tell the others you're okay. You are really popular... for a pain in the ass."

After Bertrand left the room, McConnell took the computer tablet and played with the screen for a moment. She heard a chirping connection.

"Are you ready?" he asked. But McConnell wasn't talking to Sara. He stared at the screen.

"Yup, we're good on this side."

McConnell turned the tablet to face Sara. The camera view at the other end spun hastily, agitated, before she glimpsed something tan. Becca's bloodshot eyes looked at the screen when the camera came to rest.

McConnell handed Sara the tablet, and she put her head closer to the screen.

"Hi, baby," she whispered, tears breaking through the dams in her eyes. One weakened thud from Becca's tail answered Sara's words.

"Sergeant O'Shea," a woman said from the other end of the connection. "I'm Dr. Simpson. I was the lead surgeon on Becca. She's going to be in recovery for some time, and we'll need to keep her here for a while. The bullet hit her liver and hung around the area for a bit before we could get it out. She's going to stay here until I think she can leave. Maybe a month or more. There will be follow-up therapy, but I think our girl is going to fully recover."

Becca blinked lazily at Sara through the camera. Sara's fingertips touched the screen, vainly trying to stroke that muzzle.

"Thank you, Dr. Simpson."

"That's what we're here for," she said.

The tablet image jerked around again until it stabilized when someone propped it facing the kennel, where Becca recovered. Sara stared at it. She talked to McConnell without taking her eyes off the screen.

"How is Bernie?" she asked. There was a pause.

"He didn't make it," McConnell said. "He was dead at the scene. You killed Oliver Newkirk. As far as we can figure, he and his brother were occupying the basement rooms. That's where they set up their equipment, including the 3D printer."

"Did anyone else get hurt?" Sara wasn't talking about the bad guys. She didn't give a shit about them. McConnell sensed he knew it.

"One agent broke a finger when he attempted to open a door. William 'Butch' Wilson is dead. Gerry Harris is in critical condition here. Michel Estel is in stable condition. You, Officer Duarte, and Officer Becca were the only real casualties in the raid."

"We should have planned for a better insertion," she said, thinking about what the review board might ask when she faced the inquiries. "More officers should have gone into the basement, or not at all, barring the door from the outside. I don't know."

Sara looked up when she felt McConnell's hand on her arm. "It's alright; it's not your fault," he said. "We've got a lot to go through for a few weeks. If Sheppard ever let me off her leash, I'd have been there with you."

"Was that a pun?"

"No, but I can see why you would think that."

Sara stared at Becca sleeping inside the kennel. The veterinary staff left the monitor alone. She heard talking and movement from the animal hospital, but Becca wasn't responding to the sounds.

McConnell said something, but Sara didn't hear it. "What?"

"Peter Newkirk wasn't at the house. The other unidentified subject at the table in the restaurant wasn't there either."

"That means nothing. If Peter is the computer genius and the other brain behind the operation, that doesn't mean they were bunkmates."

"That's true. But for now, we're spinning our wheels. All the accounts our forensic teams tracked for the stolen funds all went dark. They transferred the money to cryptocurrency, and it's as good as gone. We've got a BOLO out for Newkirk. As much as we can piece together, he's in the wind with our unknown suspect. With the equipment believed to be missing from the scene, they may try to begin again. They can go anywhere."

"What about Estel and Harris?" she asked. "Don't you give those bad guys passes when they turn state's evidence?"

"First, you've got to get them to want to talk. Harris already wants his lawyer. Once Estel recovers, he'll lawyer up too."

"If he recovers."

"Right." The quiet between them allowed McConnell to collect the tablet and end the connection gently. He tucked it under his arm again. "Get some sleep," he said. "As soon as I hear anything about Becca, I'll let you know. I've got to get back to the field office. We got a few leads on Newkirk worth tracking."

"I don't care."

McConnell appeared nonplused. "Let me explain something," he said. "You're not the first cop out there that's lost a partner. You're not to blame for Becca or Bernie. Shit happens, and we learn to deal with it. As for Newkirk, we should care. From the little we've already uncovered, Oliver wasn't as computer-savvy as his brother. And you killed him. I spent a lot of time in South America and Mexico. One thing I know is its blood for blood in families. Some brothers are closer than they are to their spouses or children. If he and the unidentified subject decide to retaliate, you need to be prepared."

Sara knew better than to respond. She closed her eyes, adjusted the nasal cannula in her nose, and turned away from him. What could she say that mattered, or what did he want to hear?

"I'll be around. But you need to get better. It will be a long road to recovery for both of you. Things went sideways, but no one thought what happened in the basement was your fault. You got that?"

Sara didn't respond, didn't watch him go. The curtain swished when the private hospital door opened and closed. Alone in recovery, Sara checked her limited surroundings. They plugged her into the EKG with a PICC line in her arm. When she shifted in bed and reached down, she found the catheter the nurses had secreted into her while she slept.

How long did she have to stay? How long before she could get to Becca? Did they understand Becca mattered to her more than anyone? She'd never admit in a million years that Becca meant more to her than Officer Bernie Duarte. It bothered Sara that he'd died in the line of duty. But how could she go on if the same would've happened to Becca?

Even if the mastermind got away and Peter Newkirk wanted revenge, what could they possibly do to her?

Sara spied a plastic bag of personal property on the bedside table. Fortunately, it lay on her left, so when she rolled and leaned, pinching the bag, she could do it with limited movement and considerable pain. Inside the baggy were her lip balm, handcuff key with her shop vehicle keys, and smartphone.

Sara removed the phone and checked the battery—it was still 20%—before using her password to open it. She logged into the free hospital Wi-Fi and checked for updated news about the incident. Sara scanned the articles before her phone chirped with a text message.

The unknown sender added images. It was a photograph of Sara and Becca posing at last year's police picnic. Sara thought about responding to it but was unsure who had sent it or if the contact might open a backdoor link to hack her phone. The following picture was of

Becca alone, sitting in the grass somewhere, but she didn't recognize the location. It was a picture that wasn't familiar to Sara. She scanned the background for anything familiar. Who took that picture?

Another image showed up, causing Sara to gasp: Becca lying in the vet OR, blood and doctors all around her. She nearly dropped the phone, handling it one-handed with her left arm immobilized. She texted with her thumb and sent.

Who is this?

You're dead, came the immediate reply.

Come, say that to my face.

I was already there.

Another image made Sara want to scream. She searched for the nurse call, pulling the wired remote along the bed bar and slapping the call button. After what seemed like forever, a nurse arrived. He pulled open the curtain upon arrival.

"I don't know why they keep closing that curtain; you're all alone in here. What's wrong, dear?" he asked, seeing Sara's alabaster face.

"Get me FBI Agent Bruce McConnell. Page him. He might still be in the building. Get him. Now." She didn't scream; anger replaced the initial shock, and she spoke through gritted teeth.

The nurse left the room. Another eternity passed before McConnell rushed back into it. He was wearing an open-collared shirt and looked tired. Sara handed the phone over. McConnell stared at the haunting image on the screen. He glanced around the room. He kept the phone, reaching for his own to start another investigation.

The image haunted Sara, but she refused to let it show. She pulled the sheet and blanket up to her chin, trying to hide the goosebumps on her naked arm. Why weren't there enough blankets on the bed?

The ultimate image the unknown sender gave Sara was a smartphone picture of Sara. It wasn't from Florida at the competition, snagged from some social media site. It was a photograph of Sara in her recovery bed, asleep and completely vulnerable. The sender threatened her, threatened Becca. And that audacious image of her unconscious in the recovery suite meant he could get to her anytime he wanted.

Sare growled in frustration that there was nothing she could do to stop them while she lay in this hospital bed, forced to depend on others to protect her...for now. All she could do was quietly weep and worry and wait.

www.ingramcontent.com/pod-product-compliance
Lightning Source LLC
Chambersburg PA
CBHW052009170626

46808CB00007B/2854